To Marsha Fineberg,
With best
Personal regards

Theodor Jerome Cohen

Langhorne, PA

December 8, 2010

Reviewers said this about

Death by Wall Street:
Rampage of the Bulls

"From the first chilling moments, *Death by Wall Street* takes the reader inside the seamy nexus of Wall Street and Washington. Theodore Cohen has written the sad and tragic tale of how US financial markets and the pharmaceutical industry have 'captured' their regulators at the SEC and the FDA. Citizens beware!! Is this fiction? Sadly, it doesn't feel like it."
Mike Krauss, author of the forthcoming novel *Pursuits of Happiness*, is a columnist and commentator with a long career in U.S. government and politics, and international business.

"*Death by Wall Street* may be a novel, but beneath its surface lies a terrible truth: the US financial markets, together with a sleeping US government, have caused the deaths of hundreds of thousands of citizens by denying them life-saving treatments."
Kerry M. Donahue, Esq., Chief Counsel, *Care To Live*

"*Death by Wall Street* is a 'must read' for anyone who has ever wondered why investing in biotech stocks is not for the faint-hearted. What Cohen reveals about stock manipulation, the SEC, and the FDA, will shock you."
Ed Silverman, Editor and Publisher, *Pharmalot.com*

"Theodore Cohen, an experienced investor and respected scientist, takes us on an adventure in which he exposes the malfeasance of many on Wall Street, the ugly underbelly of hedge funds, the captured financial media, and the emasculated SEC. Strap in for a fascinating ride!"
Gregory B. Purchase, MD

"Cutting edge reporting, important insight, timely, and relevant . . . *Death by Wall Street: Rampage of the Bulls* is destined to firmly establish Theodore Jerome Cohen as a fresh voice in literary journalism."
Richard Blake for *Readers Views*

"Similar to the writing style of Michael Crichton and Tom Clancy, Theodore Cohen adheres to short chapters laying out a mental storyboard in the reader's mind. He possesses a writing style ideal for screenplay adaptation with visuals that can make for a good movie."
Gary Sorkin for *Pacific Book Review*

Other Novels by
Theodore Jerome Cohen

Full Circle:
A Dream Denied, A Vision Fulfilled

Praise for *Full Circle*

"Age is no barrier to setting goals."
Elizabeth Fisher, *Bucks County Courier Times*

"I wished wholeheartedly that it had been an
autobiography! ... It is a very enjoyable read."
Elaine Richards, G4LFM, Radio Society of Great Britain (RSGB)

"*Full Circle* is an informative and accessible story that
will be particularly enjoyed by musicians, electronic
buffs and those who delight in family stories."
Joy Ward, *The Langhorne Ledger*

"I particularly enjoyed *Full Circle* because I identify to such
a great extent with the author . . . [in music and career.]"
Edward Belanger, *Dials and Channels*, Journal of the Radio and
Television Museum

"*Full Circle* is an inspirational read anyone, including young
adults interested in amateur radio and/or music, will enjoy."
Dave Ingram, K4TWJ (SK), World of Ideas, *CQ* Magazine

Available from
AuthorHouse
www.authorhouse.com
1-888-280-7715
or your preferred on-line retailer

Frozen in Time:
Murder at the Bottom of the World
Book I in the Antarctic Murders Trilogy

Praise for *Frozen in Time*

"A nasty little piece of skullduggery
made all the more so by the fact this fictional tale
is based on real events in the author's life."
Kirkus Discoveries

"*Frozen in Time* is compelling reading, combining the
elements of conflict, suspense, intrigue, entertainment,
and enlightenment. Highly recommended."
Richard R. Blake for *Reader Views*

"If the storms make one think of Patrick O'Brian,
so does the interspersing of sea and science..."
M. K. Turner for *BookReview.com*

"A fast read, with plenty of Chilean naval history and drama on
the high seas in one action-packed novel full of big surprises."
Gary P. Priolo for *NavSource Naval History*

"If you like your fiction to read like dramatic nonfiction,
Theodore Jerome Cohen will be more than willing
to accommodate your request as he takes you to the
bottom of the Earth where you'll find murder and
mayhem blended with a dash of chilling drama!"
Deb Fowler for *Feathered Quill Book Reviews*

Frozen in Time: Murder at the Bottom of the World
Is *Recommended Reading* by Longitude® (www.longitudebooks.com)

Available from
AuthorHouse
www.authorhouse.com
1-888-280-7715
or your preferred on-line retailer

Unfinished Business:
Pursuit of an Antarctic Killer
Book II in the Antarctic Murders Trilogy

Praise for *Unfinished Business*

"Theodore Jerome Cohen . . . is a master at creating an aura of mystery, suspense, and drama. Cohen's writing style is engaging, innovative, and focused, clearly designed for the post-modern reader."
Richard R. Blake for *Reader Views*

"It was Christmas in August as the FedEx package arrived with the 2nd book of the Antarctic Murders Trilogy... [A] most enjoyable way to experience the Antarctic without having to put on a down parka."
Gary Sorkin of *Pacific Book Review*

"If you love reading a good psychological thriller and think you can stay one step ahead of a cunning murderer, you just might want to take a look at [*Unfinished Business* and] the Antarctic Murders Trilogy, a trilogy that will bring out the CSI in you!"
Deb Fowler for *Feathered Quill Book Reviews*

"Where Cohen fully succeeds is in drawing the complexity of Muñoz' character. ... With Muñoz so fully drawn, it will be a pleasure to learn his fate."
Kirkus Discoveries

Unfinished Business: Pursuit of an Antarctic Killer
Is *Recommended Reading* by Longitude® (www.longitudebooks.com)

Available from
AuthorHouse
www.authorhouse.com
1-888-280-7715
or your preferred on-line retailer

End Game:
Irrational Acts,
Tragic Consequences
Book III in the Antarctic Murders Trilogy

"… [T]o preserve the integrity of the suspense, I will simply say I was very impressed with the plot twists, especially the one which involved the Roman Catholic Church. *I should have guessed somehow these characters would be seeking a higher power to engage into their illegalities!* … As "Birds of a feather flock together," [the Antarctic Murder Trilogy] by Theodore Jerome Cohen should be packaged in a jacket and sold as a set because I certainly believe anyone hooked by the first chapter in the first novel will not be able to put this series down until all three books are finished.
Gary Sorkin for *Pacific Book Review*

"*End Game* will awaken a latent gift for music appreciation in fans of the genre of mystery and suspense while adding a whole new world of drama and adventure to the music lover. … Cutting-edge drama and suspense, revealing characters through convincing dialog, provides the Antarctic Murders Trilogy with all the elements of a cutting-edge, award-winning, best-selling novel."
Richard Blake for *Readers Views*

End Game:
Irrational Acts, Tragic Consequences
Is *Recommended Reading* by Longitude® (www.longitudebooks.com)

Available from
AuthorHouse
www.authorhouse.com
1-888-280-7715
or your preferred on-line retailer

Death by Wall Street

Rampage of the Bulls

Theodore Jerome Cohen

authorHOUSE®

AuthorHouse™
1663 Liberty Drive
Bloomington, IN 47403
www.authorhouse.com
Phone: 1-888-280-7715

This story is based on real events. All characters appearing in this work are fictitious. Any resemblance to real persons, living or dead, is purely coincidental.

First published by AuthorHouse 10/19/2010

ISBN: 978-1-4520-8499-2 (e)
ISBN: 978-1-4520-7945-5 (sc)
ISBN: 978-1-4520-7946-2 (hc)

Library of Congress Control Number: 2010913631

Printed in the United States of America

This book is printed on acid-free paper.

Front Cover Design by Chandra Rose, AuthorHouse
Book Design by Katie Schneider, AuthorHouse

Photo Credits:
Front cover photograph: BigStockPhoto.com
Dust Jacket front flap photograph of author, which also is presented on the last page of the book together with the author's biography: Susan Cohen, 2010

Copyright and Other Notices

Acronyms

24x7: 24 hours a day, 7 days a week
AM: Ante Meridiem
AMLN: Amylin Pharmaceuticals (OTC)
APB: All Points Bulletin
BCa: Breast Cancer
BS: Bulls#$%
CD: Compact Disc (optical disc)
CEO: Chief Executive Officer
CFO: Chief Financial Officer
COB: Close of Business
COI: Conflict of Interest
CPR: Cardiopulmonary resuscitation
CRO: Clinical Research Organization
CSI: Crime Scene Investigator
CSU: Crime Scene Unit
DCPD: District of Columbia Police Department
DMV: Department of Motor Vehicles
DNDN: Dendreon (OTC)
FDA: Food and Drug Administration
FUD: Fear, Uncertainty, and Doubt
GENTA: Genta (OTC)
GM: General Motors
HVAC: Heating, Ventilation, & Air Conditioning
ICOS: Icos (formally OTC; now owned by Eli Lilly and Company)
IG: Inspector General
IMCL: ImClone Systems (OTC)
IR: Investor Relations
IT: Information Technology
MBA: Masters of Business Administration
MD: Doctor of Medicine
MO: Modus Operandi
NW: Northwest (in regard to the Northwest quadrant of Washington, DC)
NYPD: New York Police Department
OTC: Over-The-Counter (Market)
PA: Pennsylvania
PC: Personal Computer
PCM: Pequot Capital Management
PDF: Portable Document Format (Adobe Systems document format)
PhD: Doctor of Philosophy
PIPE: Private Investment in Public Equity
PM: Personal or Private Message (via the Internet)

PM: Post Meridiem
PR: Press Release
PTA: Parent-Teachers Association
SEC: Securities and Exchange Commission
SOHC: Single Overhead Camshaft
US: United States
VPHM: ViroPharma (OTC)
VXGN: VaxGen (OTC; at a future date to be determined, diaDexus, LLC expects to merge into VaxGen and change the company name to diaDexus, Inc.

In memory of those who were denied
treatments that might have helped them

■

"It's all about bucks, kid. The rest is conversation."

Gordon Gekko in Oliver Stone's film, <u>Wall Street</u>

■

Charging Bull
Arturo Di Modica - 1989

**Charging Bull (sometimes called the Wall Street Bull
or the Bowling Green Bull) is a 7,000 pound bronze
sculpture by Arturo Di Modica that stands in
Bowling Green Park near Wall Street in New York City.**
Source: http://en.wikipedia.org/wiki/Charging_Bull

Future
Robert Aitken, 1935

Future by Robert Aitken, 1935
Federal Triangle
(Pennsylvania and 7th St., NW, Washington, DC)
Source: http://commons.wikimedia.org/wiki/File:
Future_(National_Archives).JPG
Picture by 'AgnosticPreachersKid'

Preface

This is a work of fiction based on real events. All characters appearing in this work are fictitious. Any resemblance to real persons, living or dead, is purely coincidental.

This book is based on three decades of experience in the world of biotechnology investing. It contains the stuff of real life, and so, you will find, in some cases, that I have cited real events, masked though they may be. But they are real, nevertheless. I have been fortunate to witness the rise of such companies as Genentech, Amgen, and others that succeeded in developing new cures for diseases that have thwarted medical practitioners and scientists since the Renaissance. Likewise, I have witnessed, sadly, the demise of companies that failed to achieve their vision of bringing 'miracle cures' to market for such diseases as cancer and cardiomyopathy, areas where even today, science is virtually helpless in the face of the relentless onslaught of Nature gone amuck. Unfortunately, I also have witnessed countless examples in which stocks of companies in the biotech universe—for example, Amylin Pharmaceuticals (AMLN), Dendreon (DNDN), Genta (GNTA), Icos (ICOS), ImClone Systems (IMCL), ViroPharma (VPHM), and VaxGen (VXGN), among others—were manipulated by Wall Street, sending the companies' share prices tumbling and dashing hopes that they would be able to raise the money needed to develop life-saving cures so desperately needed by our nation's sick. How many individuals died as a result of these immoral Wall Street practices will never be known. Suffice it to say, *the Street has the blood of millions on its hands . . . the blood of men, women, and children,* who because of unrestrained greed, unethical conduct, and immoral behavior that exceeds the bounds of a civilized society, were denied drugs that, in many cases, would have extended if not saved their lives. The Food and Drug Administration (FDA) is culpable as well. There is documented evidence of malfeasance among both government employees and special government employees—consultants serving in an official capacity—who thwarted the timely approval of safe and effective drugs that later, after hundreds of thousands of suffering patients had died, finally made their way to market. All this I have witnessed.

Writing *Death by Wall Street: Rampage of the Bulls* is how I have chosen to express my disgust and revulsion, not only with Wall Street for its treatment of the biotechnology industry, but also, with our US government for not pursuing the crooks. For it not only turned a blind eye to what the Street was doing, but also, to those who desperately needed the cures that only the science of biotechnology could have provided.

Where is the justice for those whose voices can no longer be heard? Who will speak for the dead?

Theodore Jerome Cohen
Langhorne, PA
www.theodorecohennovels.com

Acknowledgements

Susan, my wife, provided vital suggestions, insightful editing, and most importantly, unswerving support during the development of the manuscript. I could not have published this novel without her by my side. The assistance of Officer Sy Nankin, Essex County (New Jersey) Sheriff's Department, is gratefully acknowledged. Gregory B. Purchase, MD, gave generously of his time and energy to review and edit several drafts. His contributions were significant and sincerely appreciated. Finally, Commander William Alden Lee, US Navy (ret.), provided critical editorial corrections and informational updates.

One

*H*omicide Detective-Specialist Lou Martelli pulled his black, unmarked Ford 'Crown Vic' to the curb at the foot of the *Bowling Green Bull*, a 7,000 pound bronze sculpture that stands near Wall Street in New York City's Bowling Green Park. It was late winter, 2010. The weather was unusually warm for mid-March. It was difficult to miss the severed head of a man pinned to the left horn of the bull, blood dripping on the bricks below. The crimson pools of blood on the pavement pulsated with irritating regularity in the flashing light of the car's red, dash-mounted, rotating beacon.

"So, what do we have here, Michael?" Lou bellowed, using both hands to lift his left leg over the car's door jamb. Martelli had been the crew member aboard a Black Hawk helicopter that was shot down in the April, 2003, invasion of Baghdad during Operation Iraqi Freedom. Now, with the help of a prosthetic leg, he walked with a slight limp. He worked for NYPD under a special waiver issued by the mayor. "Hey," he always reminded those who asked about his injury, "at least I'm alive. That's more than I can say for the pilot and copilot, who never made it out of the chopper!" What he *never* talked about was the fact that he lost his leg attempting to save them. Lou worked hard to keep his weight down, primarily to ease the burden on his legs. But at 6-foot, 2-inches and 190 pounds, walking still was difficult. He was a big, muscular guy, the result of working out at the Dominant Fitness & Health Club in Brooklyn early every morning. But with a big workout came a big appetite, so it was a constant fight to stay away from the junk food that beckoned from the vending machine outside his office door.

"What do we have here? *What do we have here?* What the hell does it look like we have here, Sarge?" It was Michael Antonetti, a Deputy Coroner. "The Running of the fookin' Bulls in Pamplona, that's what we have here!" Antonetti was standing on a short step ladder. He had just finished taking pictures of the top of the human head. Now, he was preparing to examine it more closely before preparing to remove and bag it for evidence. A lone crime scene investigator (CSI) from NYPD's Crime Scene Unit (CSU) was busy snapping photographs of the blood-drenched bricks under the bull's head.

Martelli crossed his arms, looked at the head, and nodded. "This confirms what I've always said, Michael, if you live long enough, you'll see it all."

Lou looked at his watch. "Damn. It's 4 AM." He yawned. "I'd rather be back in bed with my wife . . . while the kids are still asleep, if you catch my drift.

"So, what can you tell me?"

"Well, what you see is what we got," Antonetti deadpanned. "Cut nice and clean, through and through, just like whoever did it was cutting up a cow or a hog. We're not that far from where some of the meatpackers are located, ya know."

Great! thought Martelli. *The last thing I need at the end of winter is having to spend time questioning people in the*

*Meatpacking District who work in the walk-in coolers and
freezers!*

"And before you ask," Antonetti continued, "*no,* we don't
have the body. God knows where the rest of this guy is. I suspect,
but of course don't know, that it has been sliced and diced by
now, with the pieces thrown into either the East or Hudson
River . . . maybe both. Whoever did this knew how to handle a
professional butcher's knife, that's for sure!

"One thing I can tell you, though . . . the head hasn't been
here long—no more than an hour. The surveillance cameras
overseeing this area should give you a whole hellava lot more
information, including the time the head was stuck here and
maybe, even, a look at who created this bit of modern art."

Martelli looked at the dead man's head. The eyes were wide
open, staring down on the Financial District, once America's
Mecca of optimism for the future of the country and the engine
of its aggressive growth. Now, the 'Street', as it was known,
was the despised source of the country's ruin . . . home to the
oligarchs who raped and pillaged Main Street while awarding
themselves outrageous salaries and stock options, their 'rewards'
for having cheated, swindled, and defrauded the Middle Class
of its savings and retirement funds.

"Any clue who it is, Michael?"

"Can't tell from what I have here, Lou. The officer behind
me spotted the head when he drove by on patrol, and he called
Dispatch. But the guy over there on the curb—the one who's
puking his guts out—may know the vic. He drove up a few
minutes ago in that white BMW. Got out, took one look at the
head, threw up, and staggered to the curb. I suspect he has a
very good idea who the vic is."

"Thanks." Martelli turned, pulled his notebook from the inside pocket of his suit pocket, and limped towards the man hunched over the curb. The guy was still spilling his breakfast onto the pavement, though from the looks of it, he didn't have much more to heave. Lou placed him in his late twenties, perhaps of medium height, with brown hair and brown eyes...no different from a thousand other men who plied the streets of the Financial District. *Whoever he is,* thought Martelli, *he's got expensive taste in clothes.* The man was dressed in a tailored Italian charcoal wool two-button suit (*Alberto Triassi*: $1450) while his shoes were of the highest quality as well (*House of Rinaldi: $780*). *Man, I'll never be able to afford clothes like that, not on a detective's salary.* Martelli knew, just from the man's appearance, that whoever he was, he certainly was no low-level brokerage house backroom clerk."So," he began, "do you always make it a practice of being down here this early?"

The man on the curb looked up through bloodshot eyes. He did not respond.

"Look, I know this isn't a good time, sir, but it would appear that you know the person on the bull back there. I'm detective Lou Martelli, Manhattan Homicide. Whatever happened to your friend—I'm assuming he *was* a friend of yours—occurred within the last few hours. And the best thing that you can do to help us catch whoever was responsible for this heinous crime is to tell me as much as you can, and as quickly as you can. In cases like this, every minute counts. And based on what the coroner just told me, we're already at least an hour behind the perp."

The man on the curb looked up, and nodded. He put his right hand on the curb to steady himself, and slowly rose to his feet. Taking a handkerchief out of his pants pocket, he wiped his mouth with it and composed himself. "You're right, of course. I'm sorry. My name's Steve Jacobs. I worked with John. . .John Williamson." The man pointed to the head on the statue. "He's. . .he was. . .my co-worker at Bartlett, Cline, and Stephenson, the investment banking and securities firm down the street. We worked as financial analysts covering the biotech universe. I had decided to come in very early this morning to catch up on my work. There simply aren't enough hours in the day to do what my boss wants done!"

"Tell me about it, Mr. Jacobs. So, about this Williamson fellow, when did you see him last?"

"We had dinner late last night at *Capricious*."

"You mean the restaurant and bar down the street?"

"Yeah. John and I had just released an analyst's report on one of the companies we follow—Polymorphic Biotechnology—and decided to catch a few drinks and dinner before heading home. We left the restaurant, I think, around 11 PM. I used valet parking. John had parked his car down the street somewhere, so we said good-bye at the entrance of the restaurant, and he took off on foot. That's the last I saw of him."

"Do you recall what was he driving?"

"Oh, yes, it's not easy to forget. He had a Ferrari *599 GTB Fiorana*. Red. Hot! I really liked that car, but it wasn't practical for me, what with me having a wife and child, and living in the City. John, on the other hand, didn't have to worry about that. He was footloose and fancy-free, as they say. The man had more women—and money—than you would believe."

"You wouldn't happen to remember the license plate of his car, would you, sir?"

"Actually, yes. It is one of those New York State vanity plates...very easy to remember. It says 'SAVE'. He told me it was meant as a joke on the 'little people'...the ones who no matter how hard they save, will never even come close to 'making it' big."

"Sounds like he was the salt of the earth, sir."

Jacobs looked down at his feet, suddenly realizing that he had painted himself with the same brush.

"Excuse me for a minute, sir, while I call the car and the plate in to headquarters."

Lou Martelli grabbed the Motorola MTX8000 police-fire two-way radio from his waist, keyed up the transmitter, and conveyed the necessary information over the NYPD secure radio network to Central. A few seconds later he heard the APB broadcast for the murdered victim's automobile on the same portable radio.

"So, you had dinner, said good-bye, and that's the last you saw of him."

"Yeah, that's pretty much it. Sorry, I wish I could tell you more. I really do. John was an arrogant sonofabitch, that's for sure, but he didn't deserve this."

"Well, someone thought he did. Let me ask you this. What did you talk about at dinner?"

"Oh, the usual. I'm a Mid-Level Stock Analyst. I worked with John covering 15 biotechs...some of the big ones like Genentech, Amgen, companies like that, as well as companies such as Polymorphic Biotechnology and Berranger Biotechnology Systems that have drugs in various stages of clinical trials mandated by the Food and Drug Administration. John was the Senior Analyst. I supported him. He was the one who told me the 'tone' we would take on any specific report we developed—positive, neutral, negative—leading, of course, to a recommendation on the company we were analyzing. . . Buy, Hold, or Sell. We could make or break a company with those reports. One of the companies we follow is Berranger. They have a small molecule for breast cancer in Phase III testing—"

"Whoa, stop there, Mr. Jacobs! I don't have a clue as to what you're talking about."

"Look. All drugs go through three FDA-mandated phases of testing that must be performed before they can be approved for use by humans. Phase I trials are intended to gauge safety, Phase II trials look at the effectiveness of the drug, and Phase III trials examine the overall benefit-risk relationship so that the FDA can develop labeling for use of the drug by physicians. The process can take up to ten years to complete. Given that timeline, you can see why it's not unusual for companies to spend billions of dollars on the development of just a single drug. Even more depressing is the fact that for every ten drugs that enter the development cycle, nine fail somewhere along the way. And people wonder why drugs are so expensive? Someone has to pay for all those failures just to get the one winner."

"I see what you mean. Okay, so, did anything unusual happen in the last month or so that caught your attention. . . anything at all?"

"Well, there was something about four weeks ago involving Berranger, which as I mentioned, is one of the companies John and I cover." He paused. "Well, at least we *used* to cover Berranger together. . . until he was murdered last night.

"Four weeks ago, at management's direction, we worked at a feverish pace to update our previous analyst report regarding the efficacy of Berranger's drug *HerDeciMax* for breast cancer. The report was released to the Street three weeks ago on Friday morning an hour before the market opened. Our preferred clients and subscribers were sent copies the night before, of course, just as we were leaving the office around 8 PM. The report didn't say anything new. Mostly it rehashed old data and information. We were told to ensure that the write-up had an overwhelmingly negative slant. The brokerage house never was positive on the drug, so I didn't give it much thought. Our specific instructions were to find fault with the Phase III data that already had been released. We were to take the position that the data simply did not support the conclusion that the drug, though safe, worked. Further, we were to imply that the final set of Phase III data, which were expected to be released within a few months, would not alter that conclusion.

"Now, I have a Master's degree in Biotechnology with a minor in Statistics. My independent analyses showed that the preliminary data *were* valid. Further, the results I developed agreed with those published in peer-reviewed journals by researchers working with the drug. Based on these results, I fully expected the final data set not only to confirm that the drug was safe, but also, that it was an effective treatment for breast cancer . . . one, importantly, that had far fewer side effects than chemotherapy. Detective, the analyses I performed convinced me that Berranger's drug extended the median time of survival by a statistically significant margin over the current standard of care. I was sure of that.

"And here's the really important thing about their drug . . . it's a 'game changer'."

"A what?"

"Berranger's drug is revolutionary. Being a small molecule, the drug can be delivered in a *pill*. Detective, we're talking about nothing less than treating cancer with a pill!

"I would have thought this to be some of the most exciting news in medicine since, well, the development of polio vaccines, especially since it appeared to me, at least, that the drug worked. And all our brokerage house did was tear down Berranger and *HerDeciMax* at every opportunity. It didn't make sense. Unless—"

"Unless, what?"

"Unless someone didn't want *HerDeciMax* approved."

"And who might that be?"

"Anyone with a competing drug for sale or with a new drug in the pipeline that was intended to compete with *HerDeciMax*. If *HerDeciMax* were to become the new standard of care for breast cancer, then any drug starting a new trial to seek FDA approval to treat breast cancer of the HER2-positive variety would have to demonstrate it was substantially more effective than *HerDeciMax*."

"Didn't you raise a red flag? Say something to anybody?"

"Are you kidding? I kept my mouth shut and my head down. In case you haven't noticed, this isn't the easiest market in which to find a new job! I'm not a fool. Not with the six-figure salary I'm making, the great benefits, and the unbelievable end-of-year bonus equal to ten times my salary.

"If the Street 'bought' our negative story on *HerDeciMax*, Berranger and its shareholders would take a tremendous beating, and any hope that the company could raise money to complete the Phase III trial for its new drug at all of the participating centers might end up going down the toilet."

"Sounds like death by Wall Street to me."

Jacobs looked down, embarrassed. "Yeah, I guess you could say that.

"But again," he protested, "that's not the position I, *personally*, would have taken. And I think my work was valid because there's another analyst at a very reputable firm down the street who came to the same conclusion I did—except *he* published it. Anyway, you can imagine how popular we are right now when it comes to Berranger's stock."

"So, what happened after the report on Berranger's drug was released in late February?"

"Well, the stock was hit hard. It had closed that Thursday night at $17.77 and held steady, within a few pennies of the closing price, in the after-hours market. On Friday morning, it gapped down on the opening to $11.99 before recovering later in the day to close at $14.94. Not a great day for the shareholders. Obviously, our report had a significant impact on the market capitalization of the company. A lot of people lost a lot of money in Berranger that day, Detective. And anyone who was 'short' the stock made a real killing. Whoops . . . that wasn't the best choice of words, was it? I'm sorry."

"Well, whether or not they owned the stock, someone 'made a *real* killing', all right, Mr. Jacobs. Now the question is, who was angry enough about what happened to Berranger's stock price—if that was the event that triggered Mr. Williamson's murder—to kill him . . . and in such a barbaric way?"

Jacobs turned pale. He suddenly realized that he could be next . . . or, perhaps, his wife or his child might be the killer's next victim. After all, his name was on the Berranger analyst report as well. He turned white, started to gag, and collapsed on the curb, sick to his stomach again. "Do you think my life is in danger, sir?"

"I can't answer that, Mr. Jacobs. The more you can tell me now, the better chance I have of finding whoever did this. Do you want to continue, or would another time be better?"

"No, no . . . let's continue."

"After the bottom dropped out of Berranger's stock three weeks ago, did you or Mr. Williamson receive any threats?"

"Oh, there were the usual number of telephone calls to our office, I was told . . . perhaps a few more than usual, with people calling us every name in the book. We're used to that. You can't win in this business, Detective. Call it right and you're a hero. Every one loves you. Disparage a stock, and people hate your guts. Call it wrong, and they want your hide. And you can never be 100% correct. No matter what you do, there are days when they want to parade you around town on their shoulders. Other days, they want to tar and feather you. But as far as telephone calls go, we couldn't care less."

"Why?"

"Because our telephone calls go through secretaries. They end up listening to the abuse. After a while, they politely tell abusive parties that their calls are being traced and that's the end it. Those types of calls *never* get through to us."

"And what about the e-mails you received? Were any of them abusive or threatening?"

"Every once in a while one will reach us from a disgruntled shareholder. We were always very careful who had our e-mail addresses. And if we received something abusive from someone whose e-mail we wanted blocked, IT took care of it for us. But I never received an e-mail that threatened my life, and John never mentioned receiving one that threatened his. People are pretty wise to the fact that putting something like that in writing could be grounds for legal action."

Jacobs wiped his mouth with the sleeve of his suitcoat. "Do you happen to have a bottle of water in your car? I need to get this taste out of my mouth, Detective."

Martelli limped to his car and grabbed an unopened bottle of spring water from the console. "Here, take this."

Jacobs twisted the cap off, took some water in his mouth, and after swishing it around for a few seconds, spit it out. Then, he drank from the bottle. "Thanks. Okay, I think I can go on, at least for a little while longer, Detective."

"Mr. Jacobs, do you know anyone, specifically, who might have wanted to kill your co-worker? Someone who lost a lot of money because of something the two of you wrote? Perhaps someone he pissed off simply by saying something negative about one of their stocks? It didn't necessarily have to be Berranger . . . it could be any of the stocks you follow. Anyone who had a grudge against him, even, say, a jilted girlfriend?"

"Oh, there are plenty of people out there who would have liked to pump a few rounds into us. No investor likes to hear an analyst say anything bad about the products being developed by 'their' company. Have you looked in on some of the investment-oriented message boards on the Internet lately, Detective?"

"No, can't say that I have. I'm depressed enough just looking at what has happened to my 401(k) in the last three years, if I even dare to open my monthly statements. The last thing I want to make time for is reading about other people's problems."

"Well, you're probably better off not doing that. Some of the people on the boards are doozies. They take everything

personally. . .watch every penny move in their issues. If a stock
they own drops 2 cents, they start screaming at their company's
Investor Relations department, demanding IR issue a press release
that provides news on a drug trial or some positive material event
that not only will help their stock price recoup the 2 cents lost,
but pump the price up another cent as well. I mean, it's unreal.

"Other posters are far more intelligent. They educate
themselves, understand the technologies or drug actions
involved, interpret the results of drug trials, and so forth. If
they have the patience, they'll explain what they know to others
on the message boards. But sometimes, the 'noise' drowns out
their messages, and often, the voices of reason not only are
silenced, but leave the boards as well. I've seen it happen, time
and time again.

"And then you have people on the message boards who are
just there to disrupt everything. Some of them simply take joy
in making others miserable. They need serious medical help to
correct their psychoses. The only ones sicker already are in the
State's mental hospitals."

"I don't know about that, Mr. Jacobs. I see plenty of that
type on the streets of New York every day!"

"Yeah, ain't that the truth? But you also find people on these
message boards whose sole job it is to disrupt the boards. They
are hired, for example, by hedge funds or other large pools of
money. Their job is to instill fear, uncertainty, and doubt—it's
called 'FUD'—in ways that scare the retail trade—the 'little
people'—into selling their holdings at depressed prices. The
people spreading FUD want to drive down a stock's price
because their employers are 'short' the stock—that is, they will
borrow stock in a company and then, sell those shares with

the intent of repurchasing them later at a lower price. Their employers need to have the price driven lower if they are going to make money. Hell, given the way the markets are today and the lax oversight by the SEC—did you see that recently, some high-level SEC employees were caught watching pornography on their screens[1] instead of monitoring what was going on in the markets?—some short sellers even sell stocks short without going to the trouble of borrowing the shares beforehand. It's called 'naked short selling'."

Martelli's head was spinning. His eyes were starting to glaze over. But he let the analyst ramble on. *Scheesch . . .* he thought, *there has to be a pony in here somewhere!*

"You can make a lot of money in biotechs by playing these games, Detective. In the field of biotechnology, failures are more the norm than the exception, believe me. You can make more money betting *against* a biotech company succeeding than on the possibility it will bring a product to market.

"Which is why the stocks in the biotech universe take investors for a real ride. These stocks are constantly being manipulated by hedge funds and the like, which bet *against* their success and lay off the risks they otherwise would incur through the options exchanges. Lots of dirty little secrets are hidden in Wall Street's closet, Detective. If John's death involves one of the stocks we were following, be prepared to open a Pandora's Box . . . a box filled with unbelievably complex and grotesque *creatures* that inhabit the investment world and that only are found within the dank fetid sewers of Wall Street . . . *creatures* that have so far evaded the eyes of the Securities and Exchange Commission. Actually, given

[1]   http://www.washingtontimes.com/news/2010/feb/02/sec-workers-investigated-for-viewing-porn-at-work/

that agency's record over the past several years, including their pathetic handling of the Madoff Ponzi scheme, that's not saying much! The fact is, though, everything I've mentioned is easily seen by any person who understands how the markets function. That the SEC hasn't moved to clean up Wall Street represents a failure of epic proportions."

"That may be, sir, but open it I shall, if it means catching the killer. One more question and I'll let you go. Can you tell me the name of Mr. Williamson's boss? What's his name?"

"'He's' a 'she', Detective! And she's my boss as well. Her name is Tricia Fournier. Here's my card. You'll find her at the same address, on the same floor. By the way, she's the one who sets our agenda . . . tells us what companies to follow, what our positions should be on these companies—Buy, Hold, Sell— why we are to take these positions, when we are to release our analyst reports, and the like. She's the one who calls the tune, Detective. I don't know where she finds the time to bone up on the things we have to know—I can barely keep up with what I have to do, and she is responsible for two other investment areas besides biotechnology. But she always seems to know what she wants and when she wants it. And importantly, she demands that we *never* do anything unless it's by her direction. I got *my* instructions from John."

"I get the picture, sir."

"Do you need me anymore, Detective? I'd like to go home and clean up. I still have a full day's work to do."

"One more question before you go, sir. Do you know anyone with surgical experience who might have known Mr. Williamson as well? Or maybe a hunter . . . for example, a deer hunter? Someone who might have had a grudge against him?"

"No, I can't say I do, Detective. Frankly, other than catching an occasional beer or late-night dinner with John, we pretty well kept our private lives to ourselves. Oh, he'd talk a lot about the women he was dating... 'brag' is a better word... but he never mentioned that he was having a problem with anyone."

"Thanks, Mr. Jacobs, I think that will be all for now. I appreciate your help. And I'm sorry about your co-worker.

"You've given me a lot to chew on. Here's my card. Please send me a copy of the report that you released three weeks ago as well as all previous reports on Berranger that you and the deceased prepared over the last two years. I may contact you later if something comes up or I need more information."

"I'll get the reports into the mail today."

Martelli turned and walked to the coroner, who by now had finished collecting fluid and other samples. He and the CSI were removing the vic's head from the horn of the bull. "I'm leaving, Michael. Please send me a copy of your report when it's completed."

"You'll have it the minute it's done, Lou. I'll bring it to you personally. I've seen a lot over the years, but never a killing like this, with so pointed a message. Human cruelty continues to astound me. And considering that this is post 9/11, this killer is audacious... I mean, really *bold,* when you think about the number of surveillance cameras we have around here. Whoever did this is angry... and highly organized. They would have to be to take the risks involved."

Two

'*I* rushed it through. Here's my report, Lou." It was the Deputy Coroner, Michael Antonetti. He dropped a 3-inch thick manila envelope on Detective Martelli's desk. It made a dull 'thud', raising some dust that climbed the shaft of light streaming into the third-floor window on the west side of One Police Plaza in Lower Manhattan.

"Man, don't you ever clean your office? This place looks like a tornado just went through it."

Martelli looked up, threw his hands in the air, and nodded his head up and down. "I need this? Did you come here to give me grief? Or were you simply put on Earth to spread joy and contentment?"

Antonetti laughed. He was a short, wiry man, with thick horned-rim glasses and thinning hair. He wore the same 'uniform' every day . . . a white shirt—open at the top with the sleeves rolled up—black slacks, and black shoes. If he owned a suit jacket, one would never know it. "You take life too seriously, Lou. Seeing people after the worst day of their lives, I figure it can't get any worse. So why not have a little fun? Anyway, if you can't jerk your friends around, who the hell can you have any fun with?"

"So, what's in the envelope, Antonetti?"

"Among other things, the color shots I took yesterday morning and the lab results of our analysis of that head we found stuck on the *Bowling Green Bull.* Here, take a look at the photos, first. Basically, you've seen everything you want to see. There's not much to add...except one interesting thing."

"And that is?"

"We did a detailed analysis of the serrations on and around the neck, Lou...where the head was sliced clean from the body. The knife used had a scalloped, or granton, edge of the type made by Giesser, which happens to be a German company. The cut was very clean, which indicates that the blade was sharp and the murderer very skilled in its use. I suspect, but don't know, of course, that the person may have been a butcher or worked in a meat packing plant. But not having any other body parts come in that we can associate with this case, that's about all I can tell you about the knife. Have you learned anything?"

"Naw. Not a thing. Nothing has shown up in the way of body parts, as far as I know. You would have been the first to see them, anyway. We *did* find the vic's car. It apparently was just where he had parked it before going to dinner with his co-worker. It's obvious that he was abducted after leaving the restaurant on the way to his car because the vehicle was found with two parking tickets under the passenger-side windshield wiper. One thing you can say about our Meter Maids...they are ever vigilant!"

Lou leafed through the other reports in the stack, stopping at the toxicology report. "Hmmm...you found a strong sedative in the vic's blood?"

"Lou, I think whoever killed him must have rushed up to him from behind—perhaps the perp was waiting in a doorway or crouched in the street, between two cars—and 'stuck' the vic in the chest as he walked past with a syringe. He used *xylazine*, a strong animal sedative. Given the quantities we measured in the vic's blood, he would have been 'out' in a second or two. I doubt the vic even had time to shout. Hell, the guy probably didn't even realize what had happened. Decapitating him was the coup de grâce."

Lou thought for a moment. "Well, that doesn't tell me much about the perp. . . could be a man or a woman . . . and could be of any height and weight. When you're wielding a syringe with an animal sedative in it, you could take down an elephant, assuming you could sneak up and surprise the beast."

"I'll tell you this, Martelli, the vic never knew what hit him. Which may be merciful, given what happened to him next. But whoever you're dealing with here has used this sedative before. That's how he knew about it and was able to acquire the drug.

"Have you been able to get into the vic's apartment yet to see if you can find any leads?"

"No, Michael, I'm waiting for authorization and some help. As you can imagine, I'm anxious to get a look at the guy's personal files, see what's on his PC, and the like. In the meantime, we've stationed an officer outside his apartment to ensure nothing is disturbed."

"Where did the guy live?"

"In a place overlooking the Hudson River. He was a high roller, all right. The vic had a two-level condominium on the 14th and 15th floors at the Regal-Standish at Riverside Place."

"Whoa! The plain-vanilla two-bedroom condos over there must start in the neighborhood of $8 million. I only can imagine what a two-level apartment musta run him. Your man was *not* wanting for anything, least of all money."

"Well, he ain't wanting for much of anything right now, except, maybe, a body to go with the head you found! And I'm trying to give him some help in that quarter. Unfortunately, given what you just told me, I doubt seriously that we'll ever see the rest of him."

"I think you're right, Lou. If the person who killed him had a butcher knife of the quality we believe he *or* she apparently used to decapitate the vic, then you can be sure the murderer also had a scalloped edge boning knife, an edge slicer...just about anything and everything needed to butcher and slice up the vic as if he were a boar hanging from a hog hook. Hell, for all we know, the perp works in a slaughter house or on a farm. Your chances of even finding the vic's 'winkie' are slim to none!"

"Michael, you are, if anything, the voice of optimism."

Martelli turned to his computer and Googled 'number of farms, land in farms, and average-size farm'. In an instant, he had what he was looking for. "Well, this should be easy. There are roughly two million farms in the United States. It shouldn't take long to figure out whodunit if the perp ever worked on a farm and butchered hogs or cattle! We probably could solve this case by lunch and be on the golf course by 1 PM."

"What are you smoking, Martelli, and why aren't you sharing it?"

"Now what?" It was Antonetti's cellphone, playing *Who Are You?*, the theme from the television show <u>CSI Las Vegas</u>.

"Antonetti! Yeah...okay...okay. Yeah, I'll get right over there. Bye."

He terminated the call and slipped the phone into his pants pocket. Stuffing his report and the photographs into the manila envelope, he tucked the package under his arm and made for the door. "I need to get over to West 104th and Riverside Drive. A guy's body was found in the bushes near that little restaurant in Riverside Park. I've been on the move all week. One of our deputy coroners is on maternity leave, and we're short-handed.

"Let me know if you find anything interesting in the vic's apartment after you get through giving the place a once-over. If you need me for any reason, you know where I live."

"Will do, Michael. Thanks for the rush job. Talk with ya later."

"Glad to help. And please...when you solve this case, promise me you'll call and let me know who the vic pissed off. Given the lab results, I'm *extremely* interested in knowing everything I can about who did this."

<u>Three</u>

'**W** addaya got for me, Missy?" It was Martelli, calling from the doorway of the lab adjacent to the City of New York's Police and Fire Command Center. Located in the basement of the Municipal Building, the police and fire personnel assigned to the Center monitored city-wide surveillance cameras and other security systems on a 24x7 basis.

Missy Dugan, a Principal Information Technology Specialist, stood five-five, and weighed a sleek 125 pounds. She wore her auburn hair in a stylish pixie cut with a soft fringe, and accentuated it with two diamond-stud earrings in the upper part of each ear. Her 'uniform' *du jour* was a pair of designer jeans and a long-sleeved chambray work shirt with the sleeves rolled up to reveal two Swatch watches on her left wrist. If they differed in time, she knew she had a problem, something neither her schedule *nor her personality* accommodated easily. Missy's great-great grandfather had been among a very few who in the early 1920s sent steel, brick, and glass thrusting skyward from the streets of Broadway into the virgin sky of Manhattan, creating embryonic skyscrapers that to this day still hold their ground against the intrusions of taller interlopers.

Though Missy's ancestor no longer plied the Great White Way, monitoring his crews' construction efforts and marveling at the ever-changing skyline of the City, the City, at least, had reclaimed his great-great-grandchild, bringing her home to the Old Man's hallowed ground. Not that the trip was without a few detours. Born in Washington, DC, Missy was a graduate of Hofstra University, where she had majored in television production. After a brief stint in Washington, DC, at a cable television station, she returned to her first love—New York City—and took up residence on the burgeoning West Side, with all its youthful exuberance, great restaurants, and wide variety of entertainment venues. A job with the City's Finest soon followed, based largely on her ability to make a reel of videotape 'stand up and walk'! The woman could work miracles. Now, Detective Martelli was going to see if she could tell him anything about what happened the night they found a head stuck on one of the horns of Arturo Di Modica's sculpture of a charging bull.

"So, Lou! Why can't you ask your perps to do their dirty work during the day? Scheesch . . . like give me a break. It's not like we have cameras every ten feet all over Wall Street."

"I'm hearing you, Missy. Give me some good news."

"Well, first the basics. The bull stands in Bowling Green Park, a block northeast of Battery Park, where State Street splits off Broadway. The building directly across the street from the statue, to the east, is at 26 Broadway. That's the former Standard Oil Building, as you know. We have a camera mounted outside that building at the second-floor level. It overlooks the bull. There are two other cameras overlooking that intersection, as well, and we have cameras along all of the side streets, so there was no lack of raw video for me to review. The one good thing about the crime having been committed at night, of course, was the fact that there weren't many people around . . . in this case, none. Except, of course, for the murderer and the head of the vic. Knowing roughly when the head was planted on the bull's horn from Antonetti's report, I was able to pinpoint *exactly* when the murderer or an accessory placed the vic's head on the bull."

"And that was?"

"2:49 AM."

"Okay, that makes sense. The vic was abducted sometime after 11 PM on the way to his car. I assume he was killed shortly after that, so add an hour or so for slicing and dicing, and another one or two, perhaps, for disposing of his body parts. It figures that the head would appear about the time you stated when you add in some driving time. And, importantly, the murderer did have to leave sufficient time for the Financial District to quiet down, as well.

"But anyone in this room could have told me that, Missy. You're the 'go-to' gal . . . the one who works miracles. You're the one with those neat TV screens that let you grab a picture, blow it up, turn it around, improve the contrast, whatever! Give me something actionable!"

Missy rolled her eyes. "You've been watching too much television, Martelli. But since you asked, whoever spiked the head on the bull *walked to the sculpture* from a vehicle parked on Whitehall Street. He, and it was a *he*—I'll get to that in a minute—carried the head in some kind of valise. It looked like it was packed in a small, white garbage bag, the kind you would use under your sink in the kitchen. I saw the perp first pull a bag out

25

of the valise, and then, pull the head out of the bag. And no . . . he didn't throw the bag into the trash, so you won't have to spend your day dumpster-diving. He put the empty bag back into the valise."

"I'm lovin' it. Then what happened?"

"Well, you saw the results. He jumped up, and spiked the vic's head on the left horn of the bull with both hands, just like he was making a basketball shot. Then, he stepped back, stopped for a moment to examine his handiwork, took off what appear to be latex gloves, stuffed them into the valise, and ran back to his car."

"Okay. Now, what's this 'he' stuff?"

"Patience, my pretty! As I said, once he planted the vic's head on the bull and stuffed the gloves into the valise, the perp turned and ran back to his car. He ran like a young man. Sprinted, as a matter of fact . . . moved along at a pretty good clip. Could not have been a gal. Guys have a different gait."

"And you know that, Missy, because—"

"Hey, in this business, Martelli, you never can do too much research. So, at the least, whether perp or accessory, you're looking for a young guy, probably in his twenties, if I had to guess. Based on the height of other objects in the pictures, for example, automobiles, I'd say he's around six feet tall. And if the guy who planted the head is actually the killer, he apparently is pretty good in the kitchen, given his carving skills. At least that's what Antonetti tells me. Maybe we could have him do dinner for us, sometime."

"You really are enjoying this, aren't you?"

"Not really. But if you lose your sense of humor, Martelli, regardless of how 'black' the situation might be, you'll go crazy. We have to deal with the worst of humanity, day in and day out.

There's no let-up. Solve one case, another takes its place. If we can't laugh once in a while, we'll end up at Bellevue."

"So, is that it?"

"Not quite, my friend. You'd think that whoever did this would take pains to cover their license plates, and indeed, the perp attempted to do this, front and back. But something happened to the cover on the front plate—I don't know, maybe the vehicle went over a bump or a gust of wind moved the cardboard that had been placed over the plate—but I can tell you this. The sedan is licensed in a state where the license plates begin with 2 or 3 numbers. I was able to increase the contrast on the plate by doing some heavy digital-signal processing, and I could see the number '27'.

"Oh...two more things. First, the left, front headlight on the perp's car is blown out.

"And second, after I improved the contrast and fiddled with the image a bit, I got to thinking that maybe, the car was manufactured in the 1980's and is a domestic make. I looked at some old photographs of cars made in those years, but I can't be sure of the manufacturer...maybe GM. Don't hold me to that. Hell, they all look the same to me, but then, I don't own a car. Besides, who the hell can afford to pay $500 per month to garage the damn thing in the City?

"So, Lou, the vehicle is from a state that requires two plates for automobiles. The first two numbers on each plate are '2' and '7', in that order. The perp's vehicle needs a new left, front headlight. And maybe, just maybe, the car is a late 1980's sedan manufactured by GM. That's the best I can do, my friend. Sorry. I really wish I could tell you more."

"You done good, Missy. I always appreciate your efforts."

Four

*L*ou was staring at a picture on his office wall while flipping one silver dollar behind another in his right hand. One coin was a worn 1882 'Morgan' minted in New Orleans. The other 'cartwheel', a 1922 'Morgan', had been minted in Philadelphia. Lou's dad, Pietro,[2] a New York street cop, carried them in his pocket until the day he died in a hail of bullets from the guns of two escaped felons he had tracked to, and mortally wounded in, a warehouse on the docks in lower Manhattan. The funeral procession that followed his father's casket to the cemetery in Brooklyn included more than 300 patrol cars from 17 states as far away as Florida to the south and Kansas to the west. When Lou became a Detective-Specialist, the *Police Unity Tour* presented him with a framed picture of his Dad. Underneath the picture was a small silver plaque inscribed with the words '*Every Name Has a Story*'. Not a day went by that Lou did not stop and think about the sacrifices his Dad and others in uniform made in the service of their state and local communities.

Suddenly, Lou became aware that someone was staring at him from his office doorway.

---

2   Peter

Martelli turned and peered over the top of his desk. "And who might you be?"

"My name is Alexa Lindsay Beauvais, but you can call me 'Alexa'. I'm a Senior Forensic Financial Analyst specializing in stock market manipulation." Alexa was a slender woman in her mid-30's. She could not have been more than five feet, eight inches tall, and had shiny black hair that fell well below her shoulders. Her coal-black eyes could drill right through a person. Now, she was boring a hole directly into Detective Lou Martelli's eyes over the tops of her fashionable glasses, which were perched slightly down the slope of her bobbed nose. "And before you ask, no, I'm not married, I have no children, I live with my mother, and I'm very happy with my life."

Martelli's eyes opened wide, and he cocked his head to one side. "Well, all right. I guess we have the pleasantries out of the way! You can call me 'Lou'." He started to laugh. Alexa joined in. Obviously, the ice had been broken.

"Come in. Grab a seat. Tell me more about yourself. I asked the guys upstairs to send me the best person NYPD had when it comes to the stock market. I want to know about your background. How did you get into stock market analysis? I don't have a clue when it comes to that stuff, except of late, the only thing I *do* know is that *I'm* not the one making money. My 401(k) took a real 'hit' in the last few years."

Alexa grabbed the chair leaning against the wall and brought it to the front of Martelli's desk. Lifting her blue wool skirt slightly so that it did not catch on her knees, she sat down in front of him. "I graduated from Boston University with a Bachelor's degree in Finance, and from there, went to Wharton for an MBA. After business school, I went to the Securities and Exchange Commission (SEC) for a while, but found the environment stifling. You can't make a difference down there. Besides, they fawn all over their lawyers, who don't have a clue how the *real* world is glued together.

"So I left and went out to the West Coast, where I worked in the securities office for a state government. This was in 2002 and 2003, when then-New York Attorney General Eliot Spitzer was doing the Federal government's job.[3] Remember? Among other things, he forced ten of Wall Street's top firms to pay $1.4 billion to settle allegations that they gave misleading stock advice to investors to help corporate investment clients. Well, I played a part in that. . . we chased one firm to ground, and nailed it, big time!"

"Spitzer was quite the hero, as I recall. Tell me about what happened."

"Well, in one case, Spitzer received a tip from a private investor that one brokerage house had issued an analyst report on the eve of options expiration. The investor—by the way, he gave the same information to the SEC, but they didn't even respond to him—claimed that the release of the analyst report was timed to cause the stock to drop so that the brokerage house would not suffer losses from options positions it had failed to close out prior to the date these options were set to expire."

"Whoa, Alexa. That sounds a lot like what the co-worker of the vic whose head we found on the bull the other night was talking about. A little more in the way of an explanation, please."

---

3   http://en.wikipedia.org/wiki/List_of_cases_of_Attorney_General_
Eliot_Spitzer

"Sorry, Lou. I get carried away, sometimes. Here's what happened.

"The brokerage house of interest facilitated some short sales earlier in the year—"

"Whoa, whoa, whoa. The vic's co-worker brought that term up, and I didn't want to stop him, given that I wasn't sure he'd make it too much longer before starting to puke his guts out again. But I really need to understand what the hell he was talking about. He mentioned two terms: 'short selling', and 'naked short selling'. What the hell are they in 25 words or less?"

"Okay, look, Lou, this may take a few more words than that, but let's say someone owns 100 shares of Martelli Firearms. I, as a stock trader, think Martelli Firearms is going to tank, and I want to profit from it. So, I tell my broker I want to sell 100 shares of Martelli Firearms 'short'. What he has to do is *borrow* those shares from the account of someone who owns Martelli Firearms stock, which the broker can do. He may or may not pay the person from whom he borrows the shares a fee, depending on how much of a demand there is from short sellers for Martelli Firearms stock. But now that he's borrowed the 100 shares, he sells them 'short' out of my account. I get the money from the sale. Remember, though, I still have to replace those 100 shares in the other guy's account.

"Here's where it gets interesting. For me to make money, Martelli Firearms' share price has to drop. When it does, I buy the stock back to replace the shares my broker borrowed. My profit is the difference between what I received for the 100 shares when my broker sold the stock 'short' and what it cost me to buy the stock back—ignoring commissions, of course."

"Okay...that's pretty easy. I guess that serves a purpose...could keep stocks from getting overheated by letting those who think people are being too optimistic take advantage of what Greenspan might call 'irrational exuberance'."

"Right. Except let's say that you, the 'short seller', aren't satisfied with letting the markets function in their normal fashion?"

"What are you talking about?"

"Let's say that you don't want to wait for normal market forces to work their magic and bring down the share price of Martelli Firearms' stock...that you want your profit sooner than later. What do you do?"

"I haven't a clue. Is there something people *can* do?"

"You bet, and it's done all the time. The hedge funds and other large pools of money gang up on a stock, so to speak...put out misinformation...hell, downright lies, if necessary...to cause the share price to drop. They leak fictional stories and drop vicious rumors about non-existent problems at Martelli Firearms—they call it 'creating a fiction'—to friends in the media, who we call 'captured journalists'. The intent is to create a negative 'buzz', forcing the stock into a vicious down-cycle.[4][5] Actually, these so-called 'journalists' are nothing but whores who would sell their *and* their grandmother's souls for a story and 'hits' on their Web sites—anything to curry favor with their sources and set themselves up for the next rumor. So, down goes Martelli Firearms. You and I, the 'little people' on the Street, panic and sell. By the time the smoke clears and everyone learns

4   http://www.youtube.com/watch?v=HRaoB34jMOQ
5   http://antisocialmedia.net/antisocial-multimedia/jim-cramer-on-market-manipulation-in-his-own-words/

that the rumors were just that—rumors—we're left with losses while the Big Guns on Wall Street, having bought up our stock on the cheap, close out their short positions at huge profits.

"Hedge funds and others also create what are called 'bear raids', where they collude and sell large volumes of a company's stock into the market at the same time to trigger the automated systems into taking the stock down. You can get downdrafts of unbelievable proportions. I saw one bear raid in April of 2009 where the share price of a small biotechnology company went from $24.50 to $7.50 in 75 seconds!"[6]

"What? *What!* For God's sake, didn't the authorities step in?"

"Hard to believe, isn't it? The people responsible for overseeing the Over the Counter (OTC) market, who really need to 'grow a pair', spent all of an hour or two contemplating their navels and then, they let all of the trades stand."

"And the SEC?"

"The SEC? *The SEC?* They did nothing, either. So, a private investor, in the fall of 2009, filed a formal complaint against the agency's Enforcement Division with the SEC's Office of the Inspector General.[7] Six months later, the IG 'punted' to . . . you're going to love this . . . *the guy who runs the SEC's Enforcement Division*—the 'fox' that was supposed to be guarding the 'hen house'."

"What?"

"Well, the Enforcement Division had received a formal request for a similar investigation from the US Congress . . . the Senate Finance Committee,[8] to be exact. So, passing the buck

6   http://www.businessweek.com/investing/insights/blog/
     archives/2009/04/dendreons_mysterious_trade.html
7   OIG http://www.sec-oig.gov/Reports/Semiannual/2009/semifall09.
     pdf p. 98
8   http://www.sec-oig.gov/Reports/Semiannual/2010/semiapr10.pdf p. 73

to the Enforcement Division was an easiest way for the SEC's IG to let himself off the hook."

"What do you mean?"

"Look Lou, given what I know about people in the Federal government and their need to cover their asses at all times, my guess is that the people at the highest levels within the Commission shut down the IG's investigation to eliminate further embarrassment to the agency. Remember, they were still licking their wounds from the beating the people in Congress and Markopolos delivered for missing Madoff's Ponzi scheme. Passing the buck to the Enforcement Division was, to their mind, a way for the SEC IG—and SEC management—to put the investigation of the bear raid on the 'back burner'."

"So, what has the Enforcement Division done?"

"Who knows? For all intents and purposes, not much has been heard of the matter since then.[9]

"The fact is, Lou, both the SEC and the people who oversee the OTC market are as useless as a toothless Doberman Pinscher on *Sominex*! But Congress hasn't been much better, either. They never follow through on anything unless it will offer them an opportunity to pander to the American public!"

Alexa was just getting warmed up. "Now, here's something that *really* will make you sick, Lou! For years, the Street has been trying to drive the same company that was the subject of the 2009 bear raid *out of business.* They forced the stock so low at one point that the company couldn't raise the money it needed to fund FDA trials for two different drugs at the same time. In the end, they had to abandon the trials for one. How many lives will *that* eventually cost?

9   http://www.reuters.com/article/idUSTRE6283ZI20100309

"And listen to this. When short sellers succeed in driving any company into the ground—I don't mean just driving a company's share price to twenty cents and forcing the company onto the Pink Sheets,[10] I mean driving the company *completely out of business*—the short sellers *never* have to close out their positions. *Never! Ever!* As a result, they get to keep all the money they made on the initial short sale, *tax free!*"

"But given the problems we have with the budget, wouldn't Congress close that loophole?"

"You would think so. Several congressmen introduced legislation in the past to address the issue, but it went nowhere. Apparently, our esteemed congressmen and senators are more concerned about keeping the money coming into *their* coffers than helping to solve the deficit problem."

Martelli sat, a disgusted, disbelieving look on his face. Then, he took a deep breath. "So, what's 'naked short selling' all about?"

"Ah, that's an entirely different animal, and one that is far more deadly. In naked short selling, sellers don't even bother borrowing the stock first. They just flood the market with counterfeit shares. The people buying the shares the other party is selling short, naked, can't tell the difference. Now, by law, sellers—that is, their brokers—have three days to deliver the shares. When they don't, you have what's called a 'failure to deliver'. Sometimes naked short sellers will eventually borrow shares from others for delivery, and then, they will turn right around and sell the same stock short, naked, again. It's a game of musical shares to them. All illegal, of course, but its widespread and, again, the rules against the practice are poorly enforced.

---

10 http://en.wikipedia.org/wiki/Pink_Sheets

"And, oh, by the way, if it will make you feel any better, by one estimate, naked short selling on Wall Street results in tax losses to the United States Treasury of more than $1 trillion a year."[11]

"So, what you're telling me, Alexa, is that our markets are the equivalent of the Old Wild West, and the sheriff is asleep at his desk."

"Worse than that. The sheriff is at his desk all right, but he's watching pornography on his PC screen! Or touching up his resume so that he can apply for a cushy job on Wall Street as soon as the opportunity arises."

"Great. But you were just about to tell me about the brokerage house the investor called to your attention that had facilitated some short sales."

"Oh, yeah. Well, the brokerage house, which had sold short some stock for a client, had taken the other side of the trade— that is, *the house* acted as the buyer. They did this in order to support the price of the stock so their short-selling client got the best execution. The brokerage house, in turn, ended up with a bunch of stock they didn't want. To hedge, they sold in-the-money call options at a forward-dated contract. They happened to be May 15's in this case. While this is not a hedge in the classic sense of the word—buying puts is the traditional hedge—it generated cash for them to offset the expenditure of buying shares.

"When the brokerage house's trading desk was sure its clients didn't want to short any more stock, it started selling the shares it had accumulated, leaving the call positions open.

"When May came around, the stock price started to rise above $15. This put the brokerage company's calls in play. In

---

11   http://www.faulkingtruth.com/Articles/-EditorsCorner/1066.html

all likelihood, the brokerage company no longer had the shares on its books to deliver. If the stock price ended above $15 when the options expired, the brokerage house would have to go into the market and buy a bunch of shares to make good on the contracts. In doing so, they would have suffered huge losses.

"The simpler thing to do was to have the house's trading desk—that is, the people who execute the house's trades—work to control the stock's price and ask their stock analysts to issue a research report, denigrating the company and its lead product...which they did. And the analyst side of the house agreed to help them!

"Now, get this. The price of the stock was $15.50 on the Wednesday before options expiration. The negative analyst's report was released on Thursday morning. The stock dropped to $11 and change on the opening that day before recovering and climbing back to just under $13, where it held for the rest of the day and into the after market. It climbed a little more on Friday, but still ended up just under $15—at $14.90, to be exact—when trading ended for the week. The options expired the next day at that price. The brokerage company didn't have to buy one share at the market to make good on a single options contract. Put another way, all of the options they held expired worthless."

"My God!"

"Basically, you had a case here of the research side of the house aiding and abetting the activities of the trading side of the house. And we nailed and fined them $50 million."

Martelli shook his head in disbelief. "And this all started because a private investor, sitting at home in front of his PC, put the whole thing together?"

"Oh, yes. You wouldn't believe what's available on the Internet. If you know *what* to look for, and *where* to look for it, you can find some pretty amazing things. And you don't have to have an MBA to uncover what the cockroaches are up to.

"What's frustrating is to discover crimes like this and then, to be ignored by the Federal authorities when you present them with the evidence. I don't know whether the people in Washington are ignorant or simply lazy. But the result is the same. And even when the SEC, for example, prosecutes a case, no one goes to jail. You always see this BS about 'the company neither confirms nor denies the charges'. It's like, 'Hey, the tooth fairy is to blame!' I mean, give me a break.

"Do you know, Lou, that in the late 1980s, more than 1100 bankers went to jail after the S&L crisis?[12] Other than Bernie Madoff—who turned himself in, for God's sake—name one person from one of the big Wall Street firms responsible for the recent collapse of our financial markets who went to jail!

"In my opinion, the SEC is totally captured by Wall Street. Look at how Harry Markopolos went to the agency, time and time again, for almost ten years, with evidence that Madoff was running a Ponzi scheme.[13] Harry pushed their head in that dung heap, and they still couldn't pick up the scent. Frankly, the entire upper management of the SEC should be replaced. Hell, I think the whole damn agency should be *disbanded*! My old dog Mickey was smarter than all of the lawyers in the SEC's Enforcement Division put together! And I can prove it!"

Lou started laughing. "This I gotta hear."

12 http://blogs.alternet.org/speakeasy/2010/08/17/will-anyone-be-punished-for-citibanks-40-billion-subprime-lie/
13 http://www.jdsupra.com/post/documentViewer.aspx?fid=54539da2-994e-43b5-b271-19fbb7e723e3

"Oh, you'll love this! When I was a little girl—I think I was around ten years old, as I recall—my mother used to drive me to a dance school on the west side of Milwaukee every Tuesday afternoon after school. The woman who lived next to the dance studio bred dogs as a way of making a little extra money. One night, I came out of dance class and my mother handed me a little paper bag. In it was a puppy. While I was in class, my mother had gone to the house next door and had fallen in love with the runt of the litter . . . a black half-Beagle-half-Labrador pup with a white star on his forehead and four white paws. We named him 'Mickey' after the dog my mother had as a child.

"Anyway, my dad was *not* happy. Mickey cried all night. Mom and I filled a Coke bottle with warm water, wrapped it in a towel, and put it in Mickey's box. That, and an old wind-up alarm clock, seemed to comfort him. Soon, he was sleeping through the night. But then, we had another problem."

"Oooohhhh, I can see *this* coming. I can smell it from here."

"You bet . . . he did his 'job' on my new bedroom carpet. Try as I might, I couldn't get him outside in time. Day after day, mom and I had to clean the carpet. Dad was about to go ballistic. Mom knew this. So, one day, after Mickey had once again left us with work to do on the carpet, Mom gently took his snout and pushed his nose *near* his mess, but not in it. Well, let me tell you, Mickey got the message . . . fast! After that, if he had to 'go', it was 'Katy bar the door'. You had better not get between him and the door to the backyard, or he would run over you.

"Now, Lou, for how many years did Markopolos stick the SEC's nose in Madoff's dung heap? Ten? Give me a break! And the SEC still didn't 'get it'!

"I rest my case."

The two of them laughed. "You've got a point, Alexa. It's pretty bad, all right, when a mongrel dog is smarter than all the SEC Enforcement Division's lawyers put together."

"As Markopolos said, Lou, the agency is 'captured'."

"And you know what? In his testimony before Congress, Markopolos said the same of the FDA...that it was totally captured by the industry it is supposed to regulate!"[14]

Alexa, red in the face, was furious!

"Okay, okay, Alexa. Calm down, you've got me convinced! You're definitely the person I need for this job! When can you start working on the case?"

"Today! What have you got for me?"

Martelli leaned back in his chair and reached down to the floor on his left. He had big, muscular arms, the result of those early morning workouts. The floor was covered with piles of documents from closed and open cases, some going back ten years. Martelli knew where every document was. Cleaning up his office would merely have created confusion for the next six months. Hence, what appeared to visitors as one of the most cluttered offices in the Municipal Building actually constituted what Detective Lou Martelli proudly proclaimed as 'my whole office, readily expandable, easily accessible, open-source filing system'.

"Ah, let's see...here they are." He grabbed the three-inch-thick file of Bartlett, Cline, and Stephenson analyst reports for Berranger Biotechnology Systems from the floor with one scoop of his left hand. "The vic and his partner had released a controversial report on this company a few weeks before the

14 http://www.cnbc.com/id/15840232?video=1021435842; start at 14:30 minutes into the video clip

murder. The report created quite a stir, I'm told. Let me see." He looked at his notes "Oh, yes, 'closed Thursday night, $17.77, held steady after-hours market, Friday morning, gapped down on opening to $11.99, recovered later, closed at $14.94.'"

Alexa's eyes opened wide. "Damn! That must have pissed a few people off."

"I guess so. It certainly would have ruined my day. What I need to know is, what can you tell me about these analyst reports? The co-worker I interviewed said he and his partner, the vic, were ordered to disparage this company's drug . . . but that the drug, in the partner's opinion, worked. Something's not right here. And before I go and see the vic's boss, the woman who calls the tune in that office and directed that the report set forth a negative tone, I want all the facts. Go get 'em, Lex!"

"I hear ya, Lou. I'll get back to you as soon as I can. Believe me, if there's something here that will help you, chances are good I can at least uncover a hint as to where we can begin our investigation into what the brokerage house was doing that might have played a part in the homicide. From there, it's just a matter of following the 'bread crumbs'. They always leave some behind. But I can tell you this. If your vic was involved in anything like what I've been talking about, then there probably are tens of thousands of people out there who would have wanted to kill him!"

Five

'S' teph, where are the kids?" It was morning in the Martelli Brooklyn household, where Lou lived with his wife, Stephanie, the manager of a heating, ventilation, and air conditioning shop, and their two children—a boy 13 and a girl 16. "I need to get to work, and if I'm going to drop them at school, they better get down here, and fast!"

Lou was *not* in a good mood. He had to fight traffic to drop off the kids, and then, rush up to the West Side to meet some detectives who would help him search John Williamson's condominium. The condo had been sealed, with a police officer stationed at the door. But the backlog of work in Martelli's division prevented him from receiving the assistance he requested to search the vic's apartment until this morning.

Lou looked at Stephanie lovingly. *God, she's beautiful—two children and 20 years, and her figure hasn't changed from what it looked like on the day she graduated from high school.* Stephanie *was* beautiful...and tough! At five-seven, she still weighed 130 pounds. With long, wavy brown hair and hazel eyes, she turned heads wherever she went. This was especially the case if she and Lou were out on the town for an evening. Then, she usually dressed in skinny black jeans that accentuated every curve, black boots, and a tight sweater that left little to the imagination. A self-taught businesswoman, she ran the HVAC shop she managed with an iron fist. More than one sheet metal worker found himself bounced onto the street—"You know what you can do with your union!"—when he dared to show up late for a job or challenge her authority.

She had to be tough to nurse Lou back to health after he returned from Iraq in the spring of 2003. What she found on her first visit to Walter Reed Army Hospital in Washington, DC, was not the man she kissed good-bye early in January of that year...neither physically *nor* mentally. It was one thing for the doctors to fit him with a prosthetic leg to replace the one he lost in the war. But it took over a year before his nightmares stopped. Night after night she was awakened by his screams as he yelled to the pilot and co-pilot of their ill-fated Black Hawk to free themselves from the debris in the cockpit and fight their way back through the flames to the rear sliding door, where he stood waiting for them. When he saw that they could not get out of the cockpit, and despite his shattered left leg and second-degree burns on his hip, Lou fought his way to the front of the aircraft, only to be driven back by the intense heat from fuel that had ignited. His last memory before he blacked out was of the cries from the cockpit...desperate cries for help that he never was able to answer...desperate cries that he heard, over and over again in his nightmares, until he thought he would go insane. It was Stephanie who always was there when that happened, soothing him, changing the bed sheets that had become drenched in sweat, and assuring him that 'this too shall pass' and tomorrow would be a better day.

Stephanie started tapping her foot. "Tiffany, Rob, get down here *now*! I'm going to start counting in a second, and if I get to 3, all hell is going to break loose."

The children, if you could call them that, knew their mother meant business. It took only a New York Minute[15] before Lou and his wife heard their two teenagers galloping down the stairs.

Stephanie brought toast to the table, and then, sat down to eat her bowl of cereal and banana. "That's better. Now, perch and eat your breakfast! I don't want you snacking on all that stuff loaded with sugar during the morning. It'll rot your teeth, and the dental insurance the Police Department provides doesn't cover squat, does it, honey?"

Lou was barely aware that she was talking to him. "Huh?"

"I said, 'your dental insurance doesn't cover squat'."

Lou didn't say anything. He was staring at an article in the back of the first section of *The New York Times*.

"Lou, honey . . . what's wrong?"

"I think we had another murder with the same MO as the one the other morning on Wall Street . . . it could be linked to the case I'm investigating. Damn, I need to look into this." He limped out of the kitchen as fast as he could, hopping at times, grabbed his cellphone, and speed-dialed one of his associates, Detective-Specialist Sean O'Keeffe. It took but a few rings for O'Keeffe to answer.

"Sean, check out page A22, top, this morning's *Times*. The DC Police found a severed head in the lap of Robert Aitken's statue *Future,* which is at Federal Triangle, on Pennsylvania Avenue and 7th Street, NW. According to the article, 'Carved

15 Johnny Carson once said, it's the interval between a Manhattan traffic light turning green and the guy behind you honking his horn.

below the statue is a quotation from Shakespeare. It reads, *What is past is prologue'.*"

"The head was identified as belonging to Dr. Paul K. Broussard, Professor of Oncology, the University of the Carolinas, and a consultant to the National Cancer Institute...in the area of advanced therapeutics for breast cancer. The article also notes that a severed hand had washed up under the Woodrow Wilson Bridge on the Virginia side of the Potomac River early in the morning of the same day on which the head was found. Based on a fingerprint analysis, the hand belonged to Broussard as well."

"That's pretty amazing, Lou. You would think that with all the police on the street down there—I mean, you have the DC Police, the Capitol Hill Police, the United States Park Police, and the various members of the military police, among others—not to mention the surveillance put in place after 9/11, it would be impossible for anyone to pull off something like that."

"You would think so, all right. But look what happened in our Financial District!

"I'll bet a month's pay that the DC homicide is linked to our Wall Street homicide. In DC, as here, they have a head but no body."

Lou thought for a minute.

"Lou, you still there?"

"Yeah, I was just thinking. I wonder if the perp's use of that particular statue, because it contains Shakespeare's quote, is a message to us, warning that he's going to strike a third time! The guy would have to be pretty smart to know about Washington monuments *and* Shakespeare."

"That seems a little 'far out', don't ya think, Lou?"

"Yeah, you're probably right. Look, do me a favor, if you would. Grab everything you can on the DC case and drop it by my office. Oh, yes, and see if you can get the name and telephone number of the detective in DC who is responsible for this case. I want to call Washington as soon as I get in. First, though, I have to do a search of the Williamson condo. Otherwise, I'd handle this myself. Can you take care of these things for me?"

"Sure, Lou. Consider them done."

"Thanks, Sean. I owe you. Bye!"

"All right, Tiffany, Rob. Get on your horses.

"Whoa . . . wait a minute, young lady. Where do you think you're going, dressed like that? What are those pants?"

"Daaaaad," Tiffany whined, "these are hip hugger jeans. All the girls are wearing them. Ann Marie wore a pair to church last Sunday."

"Really? Is that so? Well, this is Father Louis Martelli of the Church of Here and Now. You have exactly 15 seconds to put something on that doesn't show any skin, or I'll ground you for a week."

"But Dad—"

"And I have the full force of the NYPD to back me up!"

"Oh, all right. But wait for me. I don't want to have to ride the geeky bus!" She stomped up the stairs, resigned to her fate.

Martelli turned to his son, who quickly squelched his smile and buried his head in his cereal bowl. Martelli knocked his wedding ring on the kitchen table to get his son's attention. "Did I hear a comment from the Peanut Gallery?"

His son looked up, smiled weakly, turned, and leaped out of his chair. "I just remembered something I need to put in my backpack, Dad! Be right back."

Now that they were alone, Stephanie tried to calm her husband. "Lou, take it easy with Tiffany. She's getting straight A's this quarter, is running for class president, and volunteers every Saturday at the hospital. She'll be okay. And there was no need to greet her date at the door last Saturday night wearing your shoulder holster and service revolver."

"Yeah, well at least the kid had the decency to *come* to the door that time instead of sitting in his car, honking the horn. And you may have noticed that unlike her previous date with him, he brought her home at 11:00 PM—right on time—instead of at 12:30 AM, as was the case on their previous date! As I tell the guys down at Headquarters, 'You can go far in this world with a gun and smile, and sometimes, you don't need a smile.'"

Stephanie shook her head and laughed. "You are *so* corny. I wonder sometimes what I *ever* saw in you."

He smiled and winked at her. "You just like tall Italian men with thick, black, curly hair and big muscles. And I'll tell you something else you already know."

"What's that?"

"We both can't wait for the day when *she* gets married and has her own 'Tiffany'. Won't *that* be something?"

She looked at him coyly. "Why Lou Martelli, I didn't know you had a sadistic side."

"There's a lot you don't know about me, Baby.

"Okay, time to go, kids! See ya, Hon."

Six

'Detective Martelli, I'm Detective Eddy Lewis. This is my partner, Detective Mary Fitzpatrick. The chief assigned us to support you on this case."

"Hi, Eddy, Mary. I think we worked together on a case a few years ago, but my memory ain't what it used to be. In any event, it's nice to have your help on this case. It really has me baffled."

"Glad to help, Lou. All hell has broken loose down at Headquarters. The mayor is all over the chief about wanting this case solved *now*! I think he's going to be assigning Sean O'Keeffe to work with you as well. The chief is working now to juggle priorities, what with the high-society Delacourt murder that occurred two weeks ago and the homicide on the West Side weighing him down."

Eddy pulled a key from his pants pocket. "I've got the key to the condo from the 'super', so let's go in. The entrance is on the 14th floor. We're going to take any computer equipment we find, so don't worry about that. We'll turn it over to our IT people. They'll give you a complete report. If you'd like any pictures taken, Mary or I can take them. Do you need gloves?"

"Thanks for asking, but I have my own."

"Good. Let's go."

Detective Martelli and the others entered the apartment of John Williamson. It included space on both the 14th and 15th floors at the Regal-Standish at Riverside Place. The only sound heard was the ticking of a large, cherry-wood finish, Moon-phase dial, 8-foot-high grandfather clock in one corner that had just sounded 8:30 AM. "Unusual room, to say the least," exclaimed Lewis. "Looks like we have a large, open living area on this floor, including separate men's and women's bathrooms as well as a large bar and game room. No question that it was used for entertaining. The bedrooms, no doubt, are on the 15th floor. Must be nice!

"Mary, take this floor. Lou and I'll go upstairs and sift through whatever's there."

"Got it, Eddy."

The two men climbed the wrought-iron and oak, open spiral staircase to the 15th floor. They were stunned by the view of the City and the Hudson River from that height, made all the more spectacular by the floor-to-ceiling windows on two sides of the condo. "Now you know how the other half lives, Lou! Your tax money at work," Eddy said sarcastically. "Where the hell would this guy have been if Washington hadn't bailed Wall Street's ass out?

"All right, let's get to work."

Lewis immediately set about disconnecting Williamson's personal computer. He carried it to the stairs, where he set it on the floor. Entering a closet, he emptied a cardboard shoebox, which he then took to where the PC had been. There, he gathered all of the memory sticks and diskettes he could find, and carefully stacked them in the box, which he placed near the stairs as well. "I'll get the 'super' up here when we're finished. He can haul this stuff down to my car."

Martelli heard him, but didn't answer. He was going through Williamson's files, which were neatly arranged in two matching, three-foot-high, wood file cabinets. It appeared that the files had been professionally set up, perhaps by his secretary or an executive assistant. The folders were alphabetized, and in them, correspondence and e-mails progressed in chronological order, from the most recent to the oldest. Martelli started at the beginning of the alphabet, took a folder, and sitting on the floor to take weight off his prosthetic leg, went through the papers. The "A" folder yielded nothing of interest. . . mostly routine correspondence pertaining to Amgen, some analyst reports, technical papers on the company's new drug for the treatment of bone metastases, and a variety of other documents. Martelli replaced the folder and grabbed the one with "B" on the label.

It took only a few seconds to see that he had hit paydirt. The file, almost three inches thick, was entirely devoted to correspondence, e-mails, published papers, analyst reports, and data pertaining to Berranger Biotechnology Systems and their drug, *HerDeciMax*. Martelli knew that if there was anything of interest to be found, it would be in the correspondence and e-mails. Wetting the tip of his right thumb, he started to shuffle through the folder's contents, stopping now and then to scan the correspondence and e-mails as they appeared. Almost all the e-mails were from two people: Williamson's boss, Tricia Fournier, and his co-worker, Steve Jacobs.

Martelli found Fournier's e-mails of *real* interest, not only for their language, but also, their content. First, she was blunt. This was a woman who didn't mince words. . . one hellava

'Dragon Lady', no question about that. He lifted one e-mail out of the stack to read it in its entirety:

```
To: jwilliamson
From: tfournier
Subject: New Analyst Report – Berranger
Biotech
Date: Friday, February 12, 2010 8:09 PM

John,

I just got a call from Bill on the
trading desk. He has a problem. We're
caught in a bad situation on Berranger
call options that settle on Saturday,
February 20th. We're short the options.
They are in the money. Unless we bring
the price down to below $15 by the
close of business on Friday, February
19th, the company will have to go into
the market and buy stock to cover the
calls.

Need urgent analysis report that slams
HerDeciMax and Berranger. I don't care
what the hell you say in that report
so long as you move the stock price low
enough for our trading desk to control
the closing price on the options next
Friday.

I don't want to hear any excuses. Just
get it done.

Tricia
```

```
PS: This will curry favor with DM,
as well. He's working on placing PB,
a "friendly" consultant, on the next
HerDeciMax Advisory Committee later
this year. DM's wordsmithing the waiver
request now to work around the issue
of how the university pays PB for each
patient enrolled in the drug trial
of DM's drug that would compete with
HerDeciMax. TF
```

"Eddy!"

"Yeah, Lou."

"Do you play the markets?"

"No, if I want to gamble, my wife and I head to Atlantic City for a weekend. The odds are better there. But my brother-in-law does. Why?"

"Does he play with options?"

"Yeah, I've head him mention them once or twice."

"Can you call him? I have a quick question?"

"Sure. He works as an accountant downtown. Easy to get a hold of during the day. What's your question?"

"Regarding options on stocks that are traded on the exchanges, when do they expire?"

"Okay...hold on...I'm calling now. Hello, Sy? It's Eddy. Fine, thanks. Listen, we're working a crime scene and going through some e-mail correspondence. We have a question. When do options on stocks expire? Yeah, options on listed stocks. Monthly? On the third Friday? Oh, Saturday. Got it. Thanks."

"There you go, Lou. Options expire on the Saturday following the third Friday of every month. He said that prices are fixed at the close on that Friday, but the options actually expire on the following Saturday, when everything settles."

"That's great, Eddy. That's a big help. Thanks!"

Martelli reached into his back, left-rear pants pocket and pulled out his wallet. In a flash, he found his Police Benevolent Association laminated calendars for 2008, 2009, and 2010. Lou chuckled to himself. *Stephanie's always complaining about the size of my wallet...says that it rivals George Costanza's on* <u>Seinfeld</u>. *She doesn't have a clue how important all this stuff is!*

Let's see...the third Friday of every month...let's go back a year and make a list of the Fridays before the Saturdays that options settled. Martelli reached up and grabbed some computer paper from the top of the filing cabinet. Taking a pen from his shirt pocket, he made a list.

February, 19, 2010
January 15, 2010
December 18, 2009
November 29, 2009
October 16, 2009
September 18, 2009
August 21, 2009
July 17, 2009
June 19, 2009
May 15, 2009
April 17, 2009
March 20, 2009
February 20, 2009
January 16, 2009

If I'm correct, there's a good possibility that I'm going to find similar memoranda to the one I just read in the week prior to one or more of these dates, assuming that the trading side of the house needed help from the analysis side.

With the list on the floor in front of him, he thumbed through the 'B' folder, stopping to read all e-mails sent or received during the two weeks prior to the dates on his list. *Well I'll be go to Hell!* He found e-mails from the 'Dragon Lady' addressed to Williamson that directed him to slam Berranger and *HerDeciMax* in analyst reports that were to be released to their clients on the Thursday prior to the last day that options traded in October and May, 2009. Further, the reports were to be released to the Street just prior to the start of trading on the last day of options trading in both cases. *Now, let's see if Alexa confirms these dates!*

"Eddy, I think I've found something immensely important to my investigation. What would you like me to do with this file?"

"Tell you what. Here's a large manila envelope. Put it in here. I'll mark it for duplication and get a copy of everything in the file over to your office by 2 PM today. That's the best I can do. I can't let you take it out of here, Lou. Sorry."

"I understand. Copies will be just fine, as long as you bag and tag the originals, and maintain them downtown. We may need all of this material in court. This is a real 'find'. In fact—

Martelli's cellphone rang. "Martelli."

"Lou, this is O'Keeffe. Did I catch you at a bad time?"

"No, I'm up in the Williamson apartment with Detectives Lewis and Fitzpatrick. We're going through the vic's personal effects. What do you need?"

"The chief told me to help you. The mayor just left his office after demanding the chief cancel all personnel leave and put every available officer on the street to find your perp. He took me off the Leonard case...said the Williamson murder now is Priority One, and he needs something to tell the mayor, *fast!* You wouldn't believe how the press has been hounding him and the mayor."

"Oh, yes, I would. Leave it to the media to turn everything into one gigantic freak show, the kind you used to pay Ringling Brothers and Barnum & Bailey[16] good money to see. All they're looking for is something sensational to hang their hat on, even if it's some trivial aspect of a major story. Stay away from them and keep your mouth shut, Sean."

"Got it."

"Look, Lewis and Fitzpatrick will be taking everything we find downtown. I'll have Lewis call you once it's inventoried and locked in the Evidence Room. After he calls, go down there. Pull Williamson's address book and anything else you can find that'll give you leads to co-workers, associates, and friends. Start 'dialing for dollars'. Set up interviews and hit the street. I need to know if this guy had enemies, owed anyone money, did *anything* at all in the last several months that would have made someone want to kill him. Let me know what you find."

"Okay, Lou, I'll wait for Lewis to call me. Bye."

Detective Lewis overheard Martelli's side of the conversation. "Not a problem, Lou. I'll call O'Keeffe just as soon as everything is stored in the Evidence Room.

"Guess you must have hit the Mother Lode with that file folder, Lou. I think you should take the rest of the day off, with pay!"

---

16   http://www.ringling.com/

"Great idea, Lewis. I'll have the commissioner charge your vacation account!"

Martelli was ebullient. "Listen, I saw something in the *Times* earlier today—another homicide similar to the one I'm investigating—but this one was in the District of Columbia. I'm going to let you and Mary finish up here, if you would, so I can get back to my office and call down there. I really do appreciate your help, Eddy. I'll thank Mary on my way out."

"Not a problem. Take care."

Seven

'Detective Jackson? This is Detective Lou Martelli, NYPD. I guess congratulations are in order. I understand we are the proud parents of twins . . . or perhaps better, twin heads!"

Detective Jackson was with DC Homicide. The case of Dr. Paul Broussard's murder had been assigned to him. "Hi, Lou. Call me Jamar. And yes, that appears to be the case. I just finished reading the NYPD coroner's report on your vic, which our people asked to be faxed down here. Looks pretty much like the DC coroner's report on our victim, which I was about to fax to your coroner's office. Same MO. Whoever's doing this sure knows how to handle a professional set of knives. My guess is he's worked in a meat market or a butcher shop, or some place like that. Nice, clean cuts, that's for sure. Maybe they could open one of these Japanese steak places in the penitentiary for him, once we nab his sorry ass!"

"Hold that thought, Jamar! Meanwhile, my friend, you and I have a problem on our hands. And if your police commissioner is anything like the one up here in Gotham City, you must already be feeling the heat. Murder is one thing, and God knows we both have our fair share. But when someone starts planting heads in prominent places, people *really* get upset. I'm sure our police commissioner is receiving hourly calls from the mayor, which means it won't be long before *my* boss starts receiving hourly calls, and—"

"And we both know that the S#$% rolls downhill, so we're in for a real bath!"

"You bet. So, tell me. You must have cameras all over that area. I mean, the statue is located at Federal Triangle . . . Pennsylvania Avenue and 7th Street, NW, as I recall."

"That's correct. The statue actually is located on the northeast corner of the National Archives Building. And yes, we have cameras all over the place. I've had our people go over and over the video data we recorded. We do see someone walking up to the statue around 3 AM, heaving the head into the statue's lap, and then, running off towards 7th Street, NW. Pretty grizzly sight, I must say."

"Could you tell whether it was a man or a woman?"

"Are you kidding? The perp was dressed completely in black. Whoever it was pulled the head out of a white garbage bag they had stuffed into some kind of carrying case—"

"A valise?"

"Yeah, could have been. But that's all we were able to determine."

"Could I ask you this, Jamar? Would it be possible to send me CDs containing the video recorded by the cameras you have mounted around the National Archives . . . basically, the block bounded by Constitution Avenue, 9th Street, Pennsylvania Avenue and 7th Street, NW? Oh, and could we get all these data beginning at 2:30 AM and running through 3:15 AM. It couldn't hurt to have another pair of eyes take a look at the recordings. I can't say we'll find anything you haven't already seen, but who knows.

"Oh, and anything else you can send me on Broussard would be helpful."

"Sure, that's not a problem, Lou. I'll have our IT people 'burn' those CDs for you and send them by FedEx no later than noon tomorrow. Just shoot DCPD an e-mail, formally requesting the data. Be sure to address it to my attention. I'll take care of the rest.

"And I'll send you what I have on Broussard, as well."

"Thanks, Jamar."

"You're welcome, Lou. By the way, would you mind if our IT people took a look at your surveillance video? Perhaps we might be able to glean something from your data that your people might have missed."

"Not a problem. I'll have my IT specialist prepare those for you today. Just have your office send a letter to my chief, referencing this call, and requesting what you need. We'll get it right down to you. And I'll let you know if we find anything of value on the CDs you send us."

"Thanks, Lou. We'll do the same. Bye."

Eight

‘*L*ou, I know it's late in the day, but do you have a little time? I've been working on the Berranger Biotech analyst reports you gave me, and have come up with some interesting data. I thought we might be able to spend a few minutes going over the results.”

It was Alexa. She had the analyst reports prepared by John Williamson and Steve Jacobs of Bartlett, Cline, and Stephenson under her arm.

“Sure, Lex, come on in. Grab a chair. Waddaya got for me? Oh, by the way, I've learned some things, too. They might surprise you.” He had a twinkle in his eye.

“Oh, yeah . . . well, I'll show you mine if you show me yours first, smart guy!”

“Ha-ha . . . just like a woman. Give me a minute, will ya. I'll have to call my wife and get permission,” he teased as he reached into the wastepaper basket and pulled out a spent business-size envelope. Closing his eyes, he put the envelope to his forehead and, as if he were Johnny Carson's *Carnak The Magnificent,* intoned, “The dates are October 16, 2009, and May 15, 2009.”

She laughed. "Wow, you really *can* teach an old dog new tricks! I'm impressed."

"Hey, who are you calling 'old'?"

"Well, come on, Lou, you must be over 40, for God's sake," she said, winking at him. "But seriously, I *really* am impressed. That's super investigative work on your part. I came up with the same dates using these reports and an options calendar.

"I'll bet if we gathered all of Williamson's and Jacob's analyst reports as well as their e-mails—and don't forget their bosses' e-mails, as well—we'd uncover more of the same for all but the largest of the companies in their stable. There is no question in my mind that these people have been manipulating the market in Berranger and other companies' stocks for several years. The proof will undoubtedly be found in the e-mails, the analyst reports, and the price action of the stocks."

"Great, but I got a murder to solve. I'll be happy to turn this information over to the New York Attorney General or whoever can do something, but how can this help me? The City of New York isn't going to pay *you* to put the State's case together for them.

"By the way, did you know that there has been a similar murder of a medical researcher in Washington, DC?"

"No, I hadn't heard that. Have you been able to learn anything about it? Was the vic associated in any way with Bartlett, Cline, and Stephenson or with a competitor of Barranger's?"

"We don't know much, yet. I talked to the lead detective in DC this morning. I hope he can send me some information that will be useful in answering those questions. But come to think of it, you can help with that now. The vic's name was Dr. Paul Broussard. He was a biomedical researcher who worked as a consultant for the National Cancer Institute in the area of advanced therapeutics for breast cancer. Now you know as much as I do.

"But here's something that's interesting. When I was in our vic's apartment the other morning, I found a folder in his filing cabinet that contained documents on Berranger Biotech. In it was an e-mail from Williamson's boss, Tricia Fournier, dated Friday, February 12, 2010. The e-mail directed him to prepare the damaging analyst report you already read. I now have copies of all the documents in that folder. What's interesting, as I recall . . . wait a second."

Martelli swung around, bent over, flipped open a folder that was lying on the floor behind his chair, and after thumbing through some papers, pulled a copy of the sought-after e-mail from the folder and laid it on the table in front of him and Alexa. "Here, look at this postscript."

```
PS: This will curry favor with DM,
as well. He's working on placing PB,
a "friendly" consultant, on the next
HerDeciMax Advisory Committee later
this year. DM's wordsmithing the waiver
request now to work around the issue
of how the university pays PB for each
patient enrolled in the drug trial
of DM's drug that would compete with
HerDeciMax. TF
```

"My guess is that 'PB' is none other than the esteemed Dr. Paul Broussard. Regardless of whether or not that's the case, I still want to know if the vic in DC had any relationship with Bartlett, Cline, and Stephenson? For example, was he a consultant to them? Beyond that, did he work in an area that involved one of Berranger's competitors? The postscript certainly makes it appear that way. What has he written recently? What happened to Berranger's stock when something he wrote was published? Maybe he released some kind of paper or report that someone didn't like. I don't know. Use your imagination. There must be some connection here because the MO of the killings is identical. I know this isn't exactly up your alley when it comes to financial forensics. But you know your way around computers and the Internet. So, I'm thinking that this whole investigation into Broussard's killing could drift into your area *should* the trail from Broussard lead to Berranger or yet another biotechnology company."

"I see what you mean, Lou. May I have the entire file? I'd like to go over the e-mails and other documents with a fine-toothed comb."

Lou bent over, scooped up the file, and dropped it on the desk in front of Alexa. "Sure, but please make copies for yourself and return the file to me today. I need it for my own work."

"Will do. I'll also see what I can dig up on Broussard while we wait on the information DCPD is sending to you. Let's find out who this guy *really* is, what he did, what he's published, his affiliations, and so forth. I can't spend too much time on it, but if I uncover anything that suggests a tie to market manipulation, I'll dig deeper, I promise you that."

"Thanks, Lex. And I'll send you a copy of everything I get from DCPD to you as soon as it hits my desk.

"By the way, how's your Mom?"

"About the same, Lou. She has Alzheimer's. That's the reason I returned to the East Coast. . . to take care of her. But thanks for asking."

"I'm sorry, Lex."

Alexa was halfway down the hall when Lou had one of those 'palm-to-the-forehead' moments. Scrambling around his desk, he almost hopped on one leg to the door, threw it open, and holding on to the door frame, shouted down the hallway. "Lex! Lex!"

Alexa, startled, turned around, took off her glasses, and looked at him quizzically. "What is it, Lou?"

"Who is 'DM'?"

"Ah ha! The light comes on! I was waiting for you to ask me that. His name is Demetri Mihailov."

"Well, who the hell is that?"

"You're the great detective. *You* figure it out!" she shouted, as she turned about, sashayed down the hall, and disappeared around the corner.

<u>Seven</u>

'**Ms.** Fournier, I'm Detective Lou Martelli, NYPD. Thank you for making time to see me this morning. I promise I'll make this as brief as possible. But you recognize, of course, the seriousness of the matter. After all, one of your employees was murdered under the grimmest circumstances, and we can't be sure that whoever committed the crime has not targeted others in your company."

"I understand, Detective. I'm as concerned as you are about this. John was a valued employee, and we are shocked by his murder. If there's anything I or anyone else in this company can do to assist you in any way, all you have to do is ask.

"May I offer you some coffee or tea before we begin?"

"Coffee, black, would be fine."

Fournier picked up the telephone, hit the "0" button, and after a few seconds, simply stated "Coffee, black, for the gentleman."

Fournier, never married, was a woman in her early 40's. She had a beautiful ivory complexion without a wrinkle in sight. High cheek bones spoke to the possibility of plastic surgery, though if it had been performed, it was impossible to tell. Her frosted, short blonde hair reminded Lou of several beautiful celebrities he recently had seen on television. And the figure she cut in her *Andreacchi* tailored pants suit ($3,200) suggested to him that this was one lady who spent at least an hour a day, *every day,* in the corporate gym. *Probably between 4 and 5 AM, unless I miss my guess!* mused Lou. She had both a BA in Finance and an MBA, which together with her 20 years of experience on Wall Street was more than sufficient to earn her the titles of Executive Vice President and Manager, Equities Research.

"Now, where would you like to begin, Detective?"

"Well, Ms. Fournier—"

There was a knock at the door.

"Come in. Ah, here's your coffee. Thank you, Robert."

Robert, in his early twenties, looked as if he had just stepped off the runway at a fashion-house review. He was tall, muscular, and exuded sex from every pore. Though hair styles on the executive floors of Wall Street firms tended towards the conservative, Robert wore his long black hair in a ponytail. He also sported a flawless, one-quarter-carat white diamond earring in his left ear. Dressed in a grey *Battelli* three-piece suit ($6200) and wearing a pair of brown *Pietro Di Michaelaso* lace-up moccasins in crocodile ($2,500), he marked the passage of time with a *Broussard-Laurent* four-dial limited-edition wrist watch (water-resistant 'skeleton' with perpetual calendar; $43,000) secured with a brown leather band. *Hmmm,* thought Martelli, *that's not exactly what one would expect an 'executive assistant' to be wearing. Someone must be taking exceptionally good care of Robert while Robert attends to the special needs of that 'someone'.*

"Detective. Detective!"

"Oh, I'm sorry, Ms. Fournier, I must have been distracted.

"Ms. Fournier, do you know anyone who would have wanted Mr. Williamson dead?"

"I don't know of anyone specifically. The thought of it is horrifying. But I'd say there probably were several thousand people up and down Wall Street as well as across the country who were overjoyed by his death, Detective. And I suspect you already know the reason why."

"Well, to be truthful, ma'am, I'm familiar with the analyst report he and Mr. Jacobs prepared on Berranger Biotechnology Systems, the one they released to your preferred clients late on the Thursday before last February's options expired.

"That sure must have made a lot of people very angry."

"Detective, analysts release reports all the time. That's their job. They're paid to track the fundamentals of the companies they follow...drugs under development in the laboratory, ongoing clinical trials, patents, litigation, the comings and goings of management personnel, and the like. These are the things about which the Street needs to have information before informed investment decisions can be made."

"No argument, there, Ms. Fournier. But in reviewing a number of the reports developed by Williamson and Jacobs, I found it interesting that several critical of Berranger had been released only days before options expired. And their impact was significant. Don't you find the 'timing' of these reports, shall we say, interesting?"

"Not necessarily, Detective— What did you say your name was?"

"Martelli, Ms. Fournier. It's an old Irish name."

Fournier was not amused. "Well, Detective Martelli, I think if you look more closely, you'll find that most of the reports on Berranger were released on days not anywhere close to those associated with options expiration. So, how do the latter fall into whatever theory you've concocted?"

"Actually, it's more than a theory, Ms. Fournier. I believe something more sinister was going on last month than just the release of a routine analyst report."

"And that would be?"

"Well, let me be more direct. Could I ask you to comment on the e-mail you sent Mr. Williamson roughly a week preceding the release of the last analyst report on Berranger?"

Martelli pulled a copy of the Friday, February 12, 2010, e-mail from his simulated-leather portfolio and handed it to her. "There appear to be a number of statements you made in this e-mail that suggest your firm was assisting the trading side of the house in manipulating the price on the common stock of Berranger. Do you have anything to say about that?"

Fournier looked up from the e-mail. Her eyes narrowed, and her voice took on a decidedly icy tone. She took off her glasses, and looked Martelli directly in the eye. "Detective, this conversation is over. If the NYPD has any further questions for me or anyone else in this firm regarding Mr. Williamson's death, our coverage of Berranger Biotechnology Systems, or any other matter related to your case, please call our attorneys. Robert will give you their name and telephone number.

"Good day to you, sir."

Eight

'*D*emetri, we have a problem." It was Tricia. She was talking with Demetri Mihailov, MD, Chairman and Chief Executive Officer, BCaPharmaceutical Corporation, New York City, on a cellphone for which only she had the number.

"Dammit, Trish, I can't talk to you now. I'm in the middle of a board of directors meeting. If you're calling about Williamson's and Broussard's deaths, I'm well aware that we need to move quickly to replace Paul on the *HerDeciMax* Advisory Committee meeting that's coming up. I'm working on the problem. It's my Number One priority, believe me!"

"That's the least of our problems, Demetri!"

"What are you talking about?"

"A detective from NYPD was just in my office and showed me an e-mail from last month they found in John's apartment. It cites efforts we made to assist the trading side of our house in manipulating the price of Berranger's stock. But scarier was the fact that there was a 'PS' in the e-mail that talked about Broussard. . .well, at least it cited him by his initials—"

"What? Do you have a copy handy? Read the damn thing to me!"

"Wait, a minute...let me get my copy."

She switched to the speakerphone while rummaging through the file cabinet behind her desk.

"Demetri, we need to see each other, not only about this, but also, about 'us'—you and me, and what we're going to do about our lives! How much longer do you expect me to wait? Good God, man, we've been seeing each other for four years. Presidents of the United States come and go in that time! Have you talked to Elise yet about a divorce? Among the problems at the office, our lives being on hold, and now, this detective snooping around, I don't know how much more I can take!"

"Trish, get a hold of yourself! You're only going to make matters worse. The first thing we have to do is stop the approval of Berranger's drug. Once we've done that, I'll be able to address our personal situation. So far, Elise doesn't suspect we're seeing each other. I don't even want to approach her about a divorce until I've had a chance to talk with my lawyers. I need a good plan going forward...something strong so I can proceed on firm legal grounds. The last thing I need is for her take me to the cleaners and leave us penniless!"

"For heaven's sake, Demetri, you've been saying *that* for two years! How much longer am I supposed to sit on the sidelines while you run off to the Caribbean, the South Pacific, Europe, and God-knows-where with her, having the time of your life, while I'm left to do your bidding? Meanwhile, I've put my social life on hold. Unless it involves you or business, I have no social life at all.

"Listen, Demetri, I've done *everything* you've asked me to do with respect to Berranger. I'm *not* going to continue supporting you much longer. Either you tell Elise you want a divorce in the next two weeks or we're through, is that clear? And that means the end of my support to you, as well!"

"Darling. You know you're the only one I love. This hasn't been easy for me either. I can't stand being with her and her mother. God, I hate going home every night, living with those two women. It's like a never-ending nightmare. You can't imagine the plans that I've made for us, once I'm free of them both. *But*. . .the divorce must be handled *very* carefully or as I said, I could be left with nothing. And then, what would we do? Sit in a trailer park, eat beans, and make love three times a day while we watch soap operas?"

"That's not funny, Demetri, and you know it."

"Come on, Sweetheart, don't make this more difficult than it already is. Let's take things one at a time. Grab that memorandum, and let's discuss it."

"Okay. Here it is. . .here's the part that has me so upset. It's in a postscript. Dammit, I could kick myself for writing it. I start off with talking about you. . .'DM'.

"'DM's working on placing PB, a "friendly" consultant, on the next *HerDeciMax* Advisory Committee later this year. DM's wordsmithing the waiver request now to work around the issue of how the university pays PB for each patient enrolled in the drug trial of DM's drug that would compete with *HerDeciMax*.'"

"Well, this is bad, Trish. I'm sorry you put that in writing. And damn Williamson for not destroying it. It never ceases to amaze me how things like this end up causing no end of problems.

"Send me a copy of that memo *by courier*, and I'll have our attorneys get with yours. Meanwhile, don't discuss it with anyone.

"Also, have your IT personnel check your e-mail servers for *all* correspondence that might be, ah, *embarrassing* to both of us in this matter. I don't care who sent what to whom. Have IT take them off the servers *tonight!* And when I say se*rvers*, I mean both your primary e-mail server *and* its backup. Make sure they do more than just delete the files. They *must* over-write each and every memory location on both servers where the documents are stored to ensure the e-mails can *never* be recovered! Everything must be off your servers by the opening of business, tomorrow, Okay?"

"Got it."

"Also, have IT destroy copies of all 'sensitive' electronic documents they find on your staff's portable computers as well as any PCs and memory sticks located in their offices and apartments. Again...they must overwrite the relevant memory locations so that no one can recover the documents. And don't forget to have everyone shred any embarrassing paper documents *using the office shredder.* Make them bring the documents to the office so you can confirm that they were shredded!

"Everything pertaining to your staff's office and home computers, memory sticks, the shredding of documents, and so forth, must be accomplished within the next two to three business days. Understood?"

"Understood, darling. I'll take care of it as soon as we hang up!"

"Good. I'll take care of things on at my end."

"But I need to see you, Demetri. Please, Darling. It's been a week since we were together. We need to meet...and talk.

Even if it's just for an hour. Can we meet tonight? Or tomorrow night?"

"I have a thought. The board of directors will be in town for the next two days. Our meetings will finish on Thursday. Elise and her mother are leaving for St. John the following Friday morning. They'll be gone for a week. We can have the time to ourselves. Meet me Thursday night at 10 PM in Central Park. . . in the back of the Delacourt Theater, where <u>Shakespeare in the Park</u> takes place. You can get to it via the 79th Street Transverse. There's a place to park, in back, where trucks bring in scenery. It's about the only private place in Manhattan I can think of right now where we can meet, outside of the back of some restaurant. And I don't want to take a chance of us being seen together.

"Do you know where the Theater is located?"

"Yes, of course."

"Good. I'll tell Elise that I have to work late to finish up some business related to the board meeting. She won't suspect a thing. We can spend our time together planning a little vacation. I'll clear my calendar for Friday and the weekend. We'll sneak away to Connecticut for a few days."

"I'll be there, darling."

<u>Nine</u>

'R obert, when Tim from IT gets here, I don't care who is with me or what I'm involved in, I want to know. Immediately! Do you understand?"

"Yes, Ms. Fournier. I understand."

It did not take even five minutes before Tim Miles arrived in Tricia Fournier's outer office, and identified himself to her executive assistant. "I'll let her know you are here, Mr. Miles."

Fournier's executive assistant picked up the handset from its cradle, and using the same hand, punched in the number '1' on the console's keypad. "Mr. Miles is here to see you, Ms. Fournier."

"Send him in, Robert."

"Yes, ma'am. You may go right in, Mr. Miles."

"Thank you."

Tim Miles was an IT veteran, having graduated from the Massachusetts Institute of Technology with a Bachelor's degree in 2001 and a Master's in 2002. He had worked previously as a technician for one of the largest brokerage houses on Wall Street when the position of Manager, IT, opened up at Bartlett, Cline, and Stephenson in 2006. Miles so outdid the other candidates in the technical exams administered by the headhunting firm hired to vet candidates that he was offered the job on the spot...at a salary 100% higher than he previously had been making. This not only bought Bartlett, Cline, and Stephenson his talents, but his loyalty as well. With significant bonuses in his 'stocking' every Christmas, management's wishes became his commands.

"Tim, I have, shall we say, a bit of an embarrassing 'situation'."

"Just tell me what you need, Ms. Fournier."

"I need the e-mail server cleansed of all e-mails sent by, or to, John Williamson. Delete them! Make him disappear. Erase any sign that the man ever existed. I don't want any record that he ever sent or received an e-mail on either the main server or our backup server. We *do* maintain a backup server, don't we?"

"Yes, ma'am. We maintain our own backup. For security purposes, it's located off site."

"Good. Then, once you've done that, Tim, delete all messages and attachments from both servers that contain the keywords on this piece of paper." She handed him a piece of notepaper that contained a list of key words, initials, acronyms, and the like. The list included 'Berranger', 'PB', and 'DM', among others.

"You do realize, ma'am, that simply deleting a file does *not* permanently erase the file's contents from the server's hard drive. It only deletes the file's listing in the computer's directory, thereby freeing up the space in memory for other uses. But—"

"Yes, yes, of course I know that! For God's sake, man, I'm not an idiot."

"Sorry, Ms. Fournier."

"Tim, *I'm* the one that's sorry. I didn't mean that. It's just that I'm under a great deal of pressure right now. Please forgive me."

"No problem, Ms. Fournier."

"I know that we can't do much more than erase the files without pulling the entire drive and overwriting it several times."

"That's what most people think...that you need to run a bootable hard drive wiper that changes every single bit on the hard drive, from start to finish, to 'zero' so the data that used to be there are completely erased when you're finished.[17] But, as I was going to say, I can use a file shredder[18] to permanently delete the *specific* files you want erased so that there is absolutely no trace of them whatsoever on either our e-mail server or our backup server when I'm finished. Everything else is left intact. This process takes quite a bit of time to accomplish, but—"

"I don't care if it takes you all night, Tim. I want you to do it, and I don't want anyone else involved. I'll leave an envelope on your desk at the close of business tomorrow night with some cash to, shall we say, 'cover' this special project. I don't care what you have to do. Shut the damn e-mail system down for maintenance, for all I care. If anyone hollers, send them to me. Just get the job done."

"You got it, Ms. Fournier!"

"Good! And then, when you're done with that job, I want you and your people to cleanse all of my staff's portable computers and PCs, memory sticks, and other memory devices we use here or in our apartments of the same information. Here's a list of my staff...their names, office telephone numbers, and apartment addresses and telephone numbers. You can start in my office. I have no PC at home, and I'll bring my portable computer and

17   http://www.ehow.com/how_4444179_erase-files-hard-drive-permanently.html
18   http://www.hardwaresecrets.com/article/138

memory devices with me when I come in tomorrow morning. This part of the effort must be completed in two days, *no ifs, ands, or buts.* Go to my people's apartments, if necessary. Make all necessary arrangements directly with them. I'll grease the skids for you!

"Do you foresee any problems?"

"None, Ms. Fournier. We'll take care of it."

"Thanks, Tim. I think you and your team can count on having one hellava Christmas this year!"

Ten

*T*alk to me, Missy." Martelli had just walked into Missy Dugan's lab in the basement of the Municipal Building holding his coffee cup and a pad of paper. His shirt was open at the top, and his tie, though knotted, was loose. He had just come from his workout in the gym—a one and one-half hour free-weight workout that left him 'pumped' in more ways than one.

"Hey, Lou. Do you always come to work in the middle of the day?"

"Hey! With a body like this, a man needs his beauty sleep. How long have you been here?"

"All night. I had to...ah...well, I had to perform a little 'midnight requisition'[19] to get ready for our meeting this morning. Here, take a look at this. It's really neat!"

Missy was one of those geeks who loved to play with anything electronic. Her dad was an Amateur Radio operator—a 'ham'—and from the time she was in diapers, she was around radio transmitters, receivers, power supplies, coaxial cables, and various and sundry parts that were strewn about her old man's

---

19 Obtaining material without proper authority; borrowing unbeknownst to the "lender"; swiping for a "good" cause.

shack. The family purchased its first home computer early in 1980, though Missy had programmed various digital devices—in binary, no less—that her dad brought home from his lab in the mid-1970s. By late 1980, at age 13, she was into hacking.[20] As she told a friend over beer at college, "Yeah, my poor dad thought I was playing computer games on our Apple IIe one Saturday afternoon when in reality, I was breaking the security features that protected some extra games hidden in the outer sectors on a floppy." Give her an electronic device, *any device,* and within 60 seconds, she could make it work, regardless of whether or not the instruction manual was available!

"What the hell do you have here, Missy. Scheesch . . . your bench looks like the control room of a major cable news channel."

It was true. Somehow, and Missy would not say how, she had purloined—'borrowed' was the word *she* used—eight tower PCs, each hooked to its own monitor. She also had breadboarded an electronic circuit with little components that reminded Martelli of spiders. The circuit was linked to eight CD readers through miniature coaxial cables. "This will allow me to synchronize everything in time," she said proudly, pointing to the circuit. "And you ditzes upstairs think girls don't know which end of a soldering iron is hot! Let's show a little respect here."

"What's this little thing here?" Martelli asked, starting to put his finger on a small component soldered to the board.

Missy whacked his wrist so hard with her right hand that Martelli's hand instantly turned bright red.

"What the hell was that for?" he yelped.

20 The terms "hack" and "hacking" are used, among other ways, to refer to a modification of a program or device to give the user access to features that were otherwise unavailable.

"Listen, ye of sweaty hands. You'll short out everything by touching your fat, wet fingers to this board. Do you see this little surface-mount component?" She pointed to something less than one-eighth the size of her pinkie's fingernail. "It took me 15 minutes to solder it in place. If you sneeze while mounting these things, you'll blow away an entire circuit!"

"All right, all right, I get it. You don't have to get sore," said Martelli, rubbing his wrist. "So, put up or shut up, lady. Show me what you got."

"The DCPD sent up two dozen CDs containing the video from cameras at the locations you specified. Good thing you asked for all the data you did because I found something very interesting. First, of course, I checked the perp's two-point layup of the head into the statue. The time at which the head was tossed in the statue's lap agrees with what the DC police stated in their report. That's a no brainer. Just because you can tell the time the head went into the statue's lap down to one one-hundredth of a second doesn't tell you S#$%.

"Anyway, I decided to recreate the entire early morning's scene *all around the block* by hooking up each CD player to a separate PC and by syncing all eight PCs in time. That way, it would be like I was watching from above . . . as if I were the all-seeing 'spy in the sky'."

Martelli was thrilled. The anticipation was almost more than he could bear. "Okay. Okay. I follow you. This is terrific, Missy."

"Now, watch and learn, Martelli. Let's start all of the CDs at precisely 2:30 AM." She pushed a miniature surface-mount pushbutton switch on the breadboard and instantly, the eight screens lit up. The streets around Federal Triangle were seen to be quiet, with only an occasional passing car or truck. "Now, watch this monitor." She pointed to the seventh screen, the second to the last on her right. "It's pointed up Constitution, to the west. There . . . do you see it? Do you see the vehicle with the left front headlight out, the one coming east, towards the camera? That's the perp. Note the time: 2:37 AM."

"Damn, Missy, there's nothing in the DCPD report about this! I'll bet they didn't look far enough back in time from when the perp dropped the vic's head into the lap of the statue. Tell me more." Martelli took a handkerchief out of his pants pocket and mopped his brow. He was still sweating from his workout, and the coffee was not helping his situation.

"Okay, now watch here. See, he turned north on 9th Street NW, and then, right, onto Pennsylvania Avenue, NW. Looks like he's going to make a pass in front of the statue, just to make sure the coast is clear."

"This is unbelievable, Missy. I've never seen anything like it! Wait until the guys upstairs hear about this."

"Okay, my friend. Now, don't get your hopes up, but look closely at screen number three to my left. It's from a camera looking up Pennsylvania Avenue, right at the front of the perp's car."

"Missy, he's coming right towards the camera. This is great! I can see light reflecting off his front license plate . . . can almost make out the num—"

"Don't get your hopes up, Martelli!"

"What the fu— I can't believe it! What the hell is that? Does the perp have some kind of anti-photo plastic cover over his front license plate? I can't see the number. Dammit! What's going on, Missy?"

"It could be one of those plastic covers, Lou. Or, it could be glare from street lights that's preventing the camera from capturing the plate number."

"S#$%! If it's glare, Missy, he needs to be closer and approach the camera at a different angle!"

"I told you not to get your hopes, Martelli. Now, watch what happens next. It gets worse."

The screen, much to Martelli's disgust, showed one of DC's Finest making a U-turn in the middle of Pennsylvania Avenue and pulling up behind the perp. The DC policeman had 'probable cause' to make the traffic stop based on one of the car's headlights not being lit.

"What do you mean 'worse', Missy? This is great!" Martelli was ecstatic. "There should be a Motor Vehicle Stop Report on this event. I'll bet DCPD didn't send it with the CDs."

"Maybe yes, and maybe no, Martelli."

Lou chose to ignore the comment. He watched as the perp's car edged towards the curb. "Well, if the problem is glare, the car still isn't at the right angle for us to see the plate number."

Martelli began thinking out loud. "If that patrolman followed procedure, he should have told the suspect to shut down his engine and remain in the vehicle. Then, he should have called Central and provided the location of the 'stop', the make and color of the vehicle, number of occupants, and the plate number. Only after he's done all of that—

"What the fu—? Missy, look at this!" Martelli pointed to the screen. "The cop barely brought his patrol car to a stop before he exited the vehicle and walked up to the perp's car. What the hell was he thinking? What was he doing? Look at the damn video, Missy. It looks like they're chatting away as if neither of them had anything better to do with their time!"

"Guess he didn't call anything in, Martelli."

"Unbelievable. Unfookingbelievable! Think about it. The perp probably had the victim's head next to him in a valise on the passenger seat! I don't believe it!" Martelli was going berserk. "There's nothing, *absolutely nothing*, in the material they sent to us that even mentions *stopping* him, much less what they talked about."

Missy shook her head back and forth. Ever droll, she finally said, "Calm down, Martelli, or I'll have to perform CPR on you. And believe me, the last thing I want to do is put my mouth on yours! Anyway, yes, the cop stopped your man."

They continued to watch the screen. After a few minutes, the patrolman went back to his vehicle and pulled out, with the perp following him. They had not traveled more than a few hundred feet when the perp made a sharp left turn and drove up 7th Street, NW, out of range of the cameras for which Missy and Lou had data.

"S#$%, Missy! That just took away any chance we might have had of securing the number on the license plate. I'll see if I can get more video data from DCPD. Perhaps they have some cameras overlooking that street onto which the perp turned.

"Dammit, DCPD had him! *They had him!* Now, we have nothing!"

"Not quite, Martelli. Let the master finish talking." She handed Lou a piece of paper. "Here's the number of the license plate on the squad car and the time of the stop. True, the cop didn't spend much time talking to the driver. And it certainly doesn't look like the officer even called the perp's license number or vehicle registration in to Central. I suspect the perp somehow schmoozed his way out of any ticket the cop was thinking about issuing. But given the hour of the morning, the cop certainly will remember the 'stop'. See if your contact in DC can talk to the patrolman. He should remember something about the perp that can help both of you."

"That's a great idea!

"Is there anything else?"

"No, from what I could see, it looks like the perp drove around downtown for a while—he popped in and out of the cameras for which we have video, though none of the video was good enough for me to get a plate number—until he stopped around the corner from the statue on 7th Street, NW, turned his lights out, sprinted up to the corner, looped the head into the statue's lap, and took off. He showed me the same running gait as the guy in New York. Definitely a young man. Beat it out of there fast, too. I'd say he left the engine running because he took off the instant the driver's door slammed shut. And this time, unlike earlier, when he was stopped, the plates were completely covered. There was nothing to see. Not even glare from the street lights. That's the best I can do, Lou. Sorry."

Martelli, laughing maniacally, headed for the door. "Yeah, but I've got the cop's license plate number and the time of the traffic 'stop'. And that's all I need!

"Missy, you truly can work miracles. If you reported to me, I'd tell you to take the rest of the day off with pay! But you don't, so get back to work! You're using up my tax money!" Missy could hear him laughing all the way down the hall.

Eleven

"*H*ey, Lex! Gimme some good news! Frankly, I didn't expect to see you back so soon." It had only been three days, and there she was, standing in his doorway with some papers clutched under her left arm and a cup of coffee in her right hand. "Come in, come in!" Lou pulled himself to a standing position, hopped around his desk, and dragged a chair next to his so that they could sit side-by-side.

"Why, Lou, I didn't know you cared. Is this a date?"

"Hey, if anyone asks, I'm going to tell them my eyesight is going bad and we needed to sit together while we worked. You make up your own excuse." He winked at her.

"You are such a romantic, Lou. I'll bet your wife can't wait for you to come home and whisper sweet things like that in her ear."

'Hey! If it's abuse I want, I can go home and get it!

"But seriously, I didn't expect to see you so soon."

"Well, I didn't expect to get back to you so soon either. But when you're up half the night, taking care of someone who's ill and can't sleep because the side effects of her medication include insomnia, you don't get much of a chance to sleep, either. So there I was, at 3 AM on the day after we talked, thinking about this guy, Dr. Paul Broussard and what connection he might have to your vic, Berranger, and that brokerage house, Bartlett, Cline, and Stephenson. I got up and went to the computer and sent a few e-mails. More specifically, I called in a few favors from guys I knew who work at the SEC and the FDA. There still are some people in those agencies who are trying to do a good job on behalf of the American people, but their efforts often are overshadowed by the politically motivated things people do at the higher levels of the organizations."

"So, Lex, what did you ask for, if I may ask?"

"Well, if Broussard's hands were dirty, or more sadly, if he had 'blood' on them, then the place to look for evidence of malfeasance would be in any academic or other papers he authored, editorials he might have written, waiver requests he submitted together with his applications to participate as a special government employee[21] on FDA-sponsored advisory committees, and the transcripts of the advisory committee meetings on which he worked. Things like that."

"And?"

"We struck gold, Lou. The guys sent me more than I ever imagined they would. For example, I learned that Broussard had submitted a waiver request more than two years ago, which was approved, to serve on the first advisory committee the FDA held to review Berranger's *HerDeciMax*. Here's a copy of the waiver. Look at this portion."

"Hell, you can't read that. . .look at all the material that's redacted."

---

21 Consultants serving in an official capacity are known as 'special government employees' and are subject to the same rules and regulations as are government employees when participating on FDA-sponsored advisory committees.

"That's the best you're going to do without going through official channels. But it told me what I wanted to know. Look closely at what is said. First, Broussard reported that he owned 'joint stock' in a company of interest. Then he reported two grants that his university received from competing firms. Notice how he concludes his request for a waiver. 'It is unlikely that Dr. Broussard's participation in the proposed discussions of a small molecule therapy for breast concern will have a direct and predictable effect on his financial interest.'"

"Well, hell, that's debatable."

```
Dr. Broussard advised the FDA that he has a financial interest
related to the above topic that could potentially be affected by
his participation in the matter at issue. Dr. Broussard reported
that he has joint stock in ▇▇▇▇▇▇▇▇▇▇▇▇▇ at a current value
of ▇▇▇▇▇▇. Additionally, he reported that his institution, The
University of the Carolinas, Asheville, North Carolina, has a
grant from ▇▇▇▇▇▇ (competing firm). The grant is current and
his institution receives ▇▇▇▇▇▇▇ per year from 2008-2012. Dr.
Broussard receives no salary from the grant. The grant is to
study a drug in late clinical trials for breast cancer. Dr.
Broussard also reported that his institution also has a grant
from ▇▇▇▇▇▇▇ (competing firm). This grant is current and
his institution receives ▇▇▇▇▇▇▇ per year from 2007-2011. Dr.
Broussard receives no salary from the grant. The grant is to
study an investigatory drug that has potential for application
in the treatment of breast cancer. It is unlikely that Dr.
Broussard's participation in the proposed discussions of a small
molecule therapy for breast cancer will have a direct and
predictable effect on his financial interest.
```

Excerpt of the waiver submitted to and subsequently approved by the FDA, allowing Dr. Paul Broussard to participate on the first *HerDeciMax* Advisory Committee

"No argument there. Before we go any further, take a careful look at the first redacted piece of information. Notice that the name of the company begins with a 'B' or a 'P' followed by another capital letter, then a space, and then, another capital letter. The name of the company is quite long. There's little doubt in my mind the company named here is BCaPharmaceutical, one of the largest pharmaceutical companies in the US. They market the most popular drug for women who are HER2-positive. In fact, their drug is the current 'standard of care' in the United States and Western Europe.

"As for the grants from 'competing firms' to Broussard's institution, I suspect that both are from contract research organizations, or CROs."

"What are those?"

"I'll get to that in just a minute.

"Now, here's what's really interesting, Lou. Look at this press release dated six months earlier than the waiver request. I found it on BCaPharmaceutical's Web site. Remember, this is more than two years old." She handed Martelli the press release.

"Look at this line, Lou."

> BCaPharmaceutical is pleased to announce that Dr. Paul Broussard, Professor of Oncology, The University of the Carolinas, Greensboro, North Carolina, and a consultant to the National Cancer Institute, will join the Phase II trial of the corporation's drug for breast cancer, *BCa-1407,* as principal investigator and consultant to the trial lead.

"What? Are you telling me that the guy was assisting another company that competes with Berranger—and a huge one at that—at the same time he sat in judgment of Berranger's drug at an FDA-sanctioned advisory committee meeting? And this is legal?"

"You bet! So my guess is that one or the other grants Broussard cited in his waiver—and it's almost certainly the first—is funded by BCaPharmaceutical through a CRO."

"There's that acronym again!"

"I know . . . stand by.

"People on the US Senate's Finance Committee and others in government and the biotechnology industry have been railing against these types of conflicts of interest (COIs) for years, and some progress has been made in forcing the FDA to address the issue. But we're not 'there' yet. The abuses continue."

"But Broussard's conflicts of interest are readily apparent. How could the FDA allow this? Who the hell signed off on his waiver? Did the official just turn a blind eye and rubberstamp it 'Approved' with a wink and a nod?"

"Good question. The FDA's Commissioner for Policy and Planning has to approve waivers. But here's a laugh. The waivers are transmitted to the Commissioner via the Director, Ethics and Integrity Staff. Now, doesn't that just beat all?"

Alexa shook her head. "What a joke! Ethics and integrity, in the FDA, of all places!"

"Seriously, here's the answer to your question regarding how the FDA allows this to happen. Basically, the waivers submitted by doctors and others seeking seats on advisory committees never show money flowing *directly* from pharmaceutical companies to those submitting a waiver."

"What? What are you talking about?"

"Lou, the pharmaceutical industry has figured out a way to get around these pesky little problems and defeat any attempts by Congress and others to 'follow the money'.

"Here's how the scam works. It'll show you why Broussard didn't have to report any direct financial support he received from participating in the trial conducted by BCaPharmaceutical. It all has to do with how drug companies pay university-based clinicians for their involvement in clinical trials."

"This should be very interesting, Lex."

"Believe me, it is. Obviously, drug companies can't pay university-based clinicians directly for this work—ethical concerns and the like prohibit it. All medical schools probably have rules in place that disallow direct payments for the management of clinical trials, or, at least, they limit the amount of money that can be paid to a doctor.

"But my source at the FDA told me that Big Pharma has two ways to get around these rules. The first way is for a drug company to contract with the general administrative office of a medical school. The contract they put in place is essentially a 'grant' to a specific department in which the clinical trial will be operated. A variant on this method is for the drug company to contract with one of hundreds of clinical research organizations—or CROs, as they are called—to run a clinical trial. Then, the CRO will put the grant in place with the general administrative office of a medical school. Are you with me so far?"

"Yeah . . . sounds like that old shell game you can find down on Broadway. Where's the pea? Except a skilled thimblerigger can move the pea from one shell to another before the game is even 5 seconds old."

"Something like that, Lou. Now, the 'grant' funds go to cover some of the general and administrative overhead costs of the medical school. What's left over goes to the department in which the trial is run. The department of the medical school then takes this 'grant' allocation and apportions a certain amount to its own overhead. The rest is apportioned to the *investigator's group running the trial.* Finally, the principal investigator then gets his or her cut of the 'grant' funding based on an apportionment rule that applies to all doctors at the hospital, taking into account the outside funding that each brings to the medical school. *Voilà!* No *direct* payment to the principal investigator, no need to report payment from a competing organization, no conflict of interest.[22]

"Such is the world of high finance and corruption in the medical industry. Money talks and no matter how 'high and mighty' some doctors may claim to be, too many of them are corrupted in insidious ways by the billion-dollar pharmaceutical industry."

"Excuse me while I throw up! I can see where the money would corrupt the Street, but the people in the FDA and the medical community? Where are these people's ethics?"

"Ethics?" Alexa laughed. "The alley cats behind my old apartment on DuPont Circle in Washington, DC, had better ethics than you'll find in parts of the medical community, including the FDA!

"The fact is, Lou, this is a tough nut to crack. If they clamped down on this practice, nearly every influential doctor would be found to have significant financial conflicts of interest. Very few would be able to serve on advisory committees. But my God, there has to be a better way of handling these situations, especially in clear-cut cases such as Broussard's."

22 http://www.investorvillage.com/smbd.asp?mb=971&mn=249529&pt
   =msg&mid=6839249

"Okay, Lex...so Broussard was a snake in the grass. Since he worked so hard to get on the advisory committee—or better, someone worked so hard to put him there—what happened when the committee met?"

"Another good question, Lou. It's the same one I had. So I had a friend dig up the transcript of the *HerDeciMax* Advisory Committee meeting for me. These meetings are usually held in a hotel in Bethesda, Maryland. The transcripts for the meetings are made available through a commercial service under contract to the FDA. My friend obtained a PDF copy for me. There were 15 members on the panel. All except two members were oncologists. One of the exceptions was a statistician and the other was the patient representative.

"You can read the transcript if you're interested, but I'll cut to the chase. Broussard was the *only* person on the advisory committee who voted NO on the question as to whether or not *HerDeciMax* was safe. He also was one of three who voted NO on the question as to whether or not the drug demonstrated 'substantial evidence of efficacy'. That specific wording, by the way, is federally mandated. My contacts tell me that sometimes, for political reasons, people within the FDA will screw with the wording of the question on efficacy. However, astute advisory committee members usually catch these attempts to bias the vote one way or the other, and will force the chairperson to reword the question before the vote on efficacy is taken.

"So, Broussard, as expected, pushed for non-approval."

"You bet. If you read the *HerDeciMax* Advisory Committee transcript, you'll find Broussard's comments throughout the meeting to be uniformly negative and disparaging of the drug. He had *nothing* positive to say about it.

"But he's only one person, Lex."

"True. As I said, the actual votes were 14-1 on Safety and 12-3 on Efficacy. That represents a very strong Recommendation for Approval. Let's set that aside for a moment and consider a few other things. I'm going to come back to this shortly, however.

"One really sad incident occurred immediately after lunch, when the government allowed patients to speak before the advisory committee and, essentially, plead for the drug's approval. Four patients got up and spoke, including two who had been on the drug during the Phase III trial and whose breast cancer was in remission. My source told me that if I really wanted to know what happened at that advisory committee meeting—the 'backstory'—I should go to one or more of the major Internet message boards. There, he said, I would almost certainly find PMs—"

"PMs?"

"I'm sorry...*personal messages* to others over the Internet."[23]

"Okay...go ahead."

"...I would almost certainly find PMs from one or more people in the advisory committee audience describing for the outside world exactly what was being said, *as the meeting was being conducted.* He said it would be like reading a play-by-play description of a baseball game."

"So...you went out to some of the boards, right, Lex?"

---

23 A personal message or private message, often shortened to PM, is like an e-mail sent from one user to another user on an Internet forum, bulletin board system, social networking site (such as Facebook), or chat room (such as Internet Relay Chat). See http://en.wikipedia.org/wiki/Personal_message

"Oh, yes. I checked the Berranger message boards on Yahoo!, Investor Village, and Raging Bull, among others. There are several such message boards on the Web.

"And I found what I was looking for, Lou. Broussard and two others, both men, apparently dozed through all of the presentations by the patients who came to the microphone.

"Now, I have to tell you, Lou, I've been to meetings where after a big lunch, I had all I could do to stay awake. But the people who were testifying in front of the advisory committee were women who either were dying of breast cancer or whose disease was in remission. If the committee members couldn't stay awake—"

Lou didn't let her finish. "They damn well should have stood up, for God's sake, and moved around behind their chairs to get their blood moving, or backed up and leaned against the wall...they could have done *something* other than nod off. They owed it to the people testifying to pay attention to what was being said."

"You bet! Two patients got very angry and stopped their testimony to 'call out' the advisory committee participants who nodded off. The son of one of the women, who was in the audience, was downright abusive of the trio. He was escorted out of the meeting at the direction of the chairman."

Martelli could not believe what he had just heard. "That's the height of something or other when you're charged with making life and death decisions, and then, you have the unmitigated gall to ignore those who are pleading for their lives."

They sat in silence. Finally, Martelli spoke. "Do you have the name of the woman and her son? Sounds like they must have been *really* angry."

"Give me a second." Wetting her thumb, Alexa made her way quickly to the OPEN PUBLIC HEARING portion of the transcript that began on page 256. She continued down through the text, page by page, scanning for signs of conflict. "Ah...here it is. The woman is Mrs. Selma Holtzmann. There's no indication, here, as to her son's name. It wouldn't be listed because he didn't speak."

Alexa traced the text of the transcription with her finger as she read Mrs. Holtzmann's testimony, making soft *humming* sounds as her finger dropped from the top of a page to the bottom. "Wait, she mentioned that they had spent so much money on her chemo treatments for breast cancer and on treating the side effects from her chemo that she didn't have enough money to fly to Washington for the meeting. Her son Terrell had to drive her out, and they slept in the cheapest motels they could find along the way."

"So, the formal Recommendation from the advisory committee was to approve the drug, right?"

"Correct. But the FDA doesn't have to follow the Recommendations of advisory committees, and in this case, the agency did *not* give its approval. Instead, it asked Berranger for more data. That was two years ago. We're just about at the point where those data should be released. Williamson and his pal Jacobs wrote in their February analyst report—the one that sent Berranger's shares into the toilet—that they didn't expect the data to be sufficiently different from the data reviewed two years ago such that it would change the FDA's mind."

"Why didn't the FDA approve the drug two years ago, Lex?"

"That's what I want to return to. It appears that some people weren't content to let things take their own course. Yes, the *HerDeciMax* Advisory Committee meeting recommended approval, but there were people both within and outside the committee who did *not* want the drug approved. And they were willing to go to *any* lengths to stop approval."

"Well, we know Broussard was one of these people. How much more damage could he do, Lex, than he already had done during the advisory committee meeting?"

"Lots! About a month after the *HerDeciMax* Advisory Committee meeting and before the FDA rendered its decision on the drug, an unsigned editorial appeared—"

"A what?"

"An unsigned editorial appeared in one of the leading biotechnology journals. It disparaged the drug."

"You're kidding, right?"

"Lou, women aren't the only ones with nothing between their legs! Medical and biomedical journals often run unsigned editorials."

"I can't believe it! If those 'literary eunuchs' don't have the 'balls' to sign their names to their crap, why should anyone pay attention to them?"

"Well, they're not written for 'anyone'. They're written with the Street's agenda in mind. They're meant to foment fear, uncertainty, and doubt, for the most part. Many are 'plants' by Big Pharma. But once again, they scare the 'little people' and drive stock prices down when they appear. . .as did the unsigned editorial that disparaged *HerDeciMax*.

"A little sleuthing by Berranger stockholders and patient advocates identified Broussard as the author. As was the case with the report released by Bartlett, Cline, and Stephenson last month, Berranger's stock took another hit when the editorial was published. I mean, it went straight into the ground.

"Now, remember, this was over two years ago. The worst part of this whole sad episode was that the company needed to raise money at that time to continue the Phase III trial. With the stock price driven so low, it was impossible to go into the public marketplace and do a secondary. Fortunately, Berranger has one of the sharpest CFO's in the business. He did a private placement with a large venture capital firm in Japan that kept the company alive."

"I'll bet that by then, Berranger and its shareholders were becoming just a little paranoid!"

"You know what they say, Lou? 'Just because you're paranoid doesn't mean that someone isn't out to kill you.'"

"This really is unbelievable. Women are dying of a terrible disease while Wall Street is trying to put Berranger into bankruptcy, doctors are attempting to stop its revolutionary new treatment *HerDeciMax* from reaching the market, the FDA could care less about conflicts of interest so blatant you can smell their stench way up in New York City, the SEC won't do S#$% about how biotech stock prices are being manipulated, and Congress continues to play with itself!"

"I think that just about sums it up, Lou."

"What's the bottom line, Lex?"

"Broussard did *not* do this on his own. Someone bigger was behind it...someone who desperately needs to stop *HerDeciMax* dead in its tracks...to stop the drug from ever coming to market. And the only one I can think of who would want *that* to happen is Demetri Mihailov, MD, the Chairman and Chief Executive Officer of BCaPharmaceutical.

"BCaPharmaceutical's treatment for breast cancer, *BCaP*, which is the current standard of care, goes off-patent in a year. You know what that means? Not only will competitors flood the market with generic copies of the brand-name drug, but the price for the treatment will drop through the floor. And if *HerDeciMax* becomes the new standard of care before BCaPharmaceutical can field a replacement for *BCaP*, they'll lose billions and billions of dollars in sales going forward. Quite possibly, they'll *never* be able to displace *HerDeciMax* as a first-line treatment if Berranger's drug is approved. Worst case, the approval of Berranger's *HerDeciMax* could spell the end of BCaPharmaceutical's dominance in the treatment of breast cancer.

"Whoops . . . hold on, Lou . . . cellphone's ringing. Hello . . . yeah . . . okay . . . I'll be right up. Bye.

"Lou, I'm late for a meeting. We're pretty much done here. I can come back tomorrow if you have any questions. But this lays out Broussard's role in all of this, and why someone might have wanted to kill him. He didn't exactly make friends among Berranger's shareholders and patient advocates alike, that's for sure."

"Thanks, Lex. This has been *most* enlightening. What I need to do now is find out *who* was behind what Dr. Paul Broussard *and* John Williamson of Bartlett, Cline, and Stephenson were up to. Who was pulling the strings? Who was the 'puppeteer'! You could be right. It very well might have been Dr. Mihailov."

"Good luck, Lou."

Twelve

'*M*issy? It's me! The man, the myth, the legend! Martelli!" The detective was hunched over in his chair, holding the handset of his office phone between his right ear and his shoulder while using both hands and a screwdriver to work a stone out of the shoe on his prosthetic device, which he was holding upside-down between his knees.

"Martelli, who?"

"That's nice, Missy . . . real nice! And I was calling to convey the wonderful things that the DCPD had to say about you."

Missy laughed. "Oh, you're *that* Martelli. I was afraid you were the bill collector who's been hounding me." Lou could hear her chortling.

"Yeah, yeah, real cute. Well, I thought I'd let you know that Detective Jamar Jackson of DCPD said whatever we were paying you was way too low and his department would triple it. I said if he made you an offer, his department would have another homicide on their hands within 24 hours . . . *HIS!*"

"But seriously, Missy, they were blown away by what you found on their video. Jamar went back to the officer who stopped our suspect to get his story. Here's what happened. The patrolman had been driving up Pennsylvania Avenue when he saw a vehicle with one headlight burned out. He made a U-turn after passing the vehicle on the other side of the street, turned on his strobe flashers, briefly flipped on his siren, and drove up behind the car. The driver immediately pulled to the curb, and the patrolman parked behind him.

"At that point, the patrolman only glanced at the license plate, figuring he would get all the information he needed once he saw the driver license and the vehicle registration. He remembered that the first two numbers on the plate were '2' and '7', because he had just celebrated his 27th birthday. He also said he *thought* he saw a farm scene on the license plate, but other than that, he couldn't recall anything.

"For some unknown reason—and Jamar said that the guy's supervisor is going to have a 'little chat' with the patrolman about this—the officer completely broke protocol on this 'stop'. For a single-man unit *not* to call Central, especially at that hour of the morning on a deserted street, is totally against Department regulations. But he did it. It's done.

"Anyway, Jamar said the driver opened his window as the patrolman walked up to the vehicle and the young man—the officer put him in his mid- to late 20s—immediately started to bemoan the fact that he was totally lost. The driver said he had been to Rehoboth Beach, Delaware, with some friends, and now, was driving home to the Midwest. He said he had intended to take Route 50 West to Washington, DC, where he was going to pick up the Interstate system at the Beltway. Somehow, he missed the I-495 exit and followed Route 50 into the city. He told the patrolman that he not only didn't know where he was, but also, didn't have a clue as to what he should do next to get back on the Interstate."

"Well, Lou, I can sympathize with him. Having lived and worked in Washington, I'll be the first to say that it can be as confusing as hell. L'Enfant didn't do anyone any favors, not with those circles and hundreds of streets going here, there, and everywhere. Add a few hundred one-way streets and the large number of roads that reverse direction as a function of the time of day, sprinkle in some tourists who have no idea what they're doing, and then add a dash of idiots who seem to believe it is their God-given right to make their own rules-of-the-road, and you end up with total confusion on the roads, regardless of the time of day . . . or night! And then you have the Beltway. No wonder drivers down there shoot at each other."

"Yeah, I know what you mean. Driving on the Beltway with Stephanie and the kids almost brought me to tears once!

"Anyway, you'll love this, Missy. The patrolman said the driver told him he didn't even have enough money for a motel room . . . that he probably would have to sleep in his car that night. He said everything he owned was in the valise next to him in the passenger seat!"

"That's incredible, Lou! *The head was in the valise!* The perp probably was sitting there, patting it like it was his dog while he and the cop were schmoozing as if they were neighbors having beers at a backyard barbeque! This guy is astoundingly bold."

"I know. Doesn't that just— Anyway, the cop took pity on the guy, drew a map on the back of a pizza restaurant's napkin the perp had handed him, wished him luck, and let him go."

Neither said anything for a few seconds. It was beginning to sink in. Both were getting a very real sense of the killer's anger and of his willingness to go to almost *any* lengths to achieve whatever his motive may have been in killing Dr. Broussard and, most likely, John Williamson.

Finally, Martelli spoke. "It's almost feels like that guy *wants* to get caught."

"You'd know more about that than I would, Lou."

"Yeah, I guess so.

"Anyway, I took a flyer and went with what I had. A quick check on the Internet told me that the plate probably was from Iowa . . . that's the only Midwest state with a farm scene on the plate. And the fact that the alpha-numeric identifier on the plate begins with three numbers made sense as well.

**Current Iowa vehicle license plate:
blue on reflective white farm scene in foreground and
skyline in background[24]. This example plate would
have been issued to a resident of Woodbury County.**

"So, I had our people send an official inter-agency request to the Iowa Motor Vehicle Division in Des Moines, seeking a CD with all of the vehicle registrations, current *and* cancelled,

---

24 http://en.wikipedia.org/wiki/United_States_license_plate_
designs_and_serial_formats

for automobiles that begin with '27'. We should have it in a few days."

"Well, Martelli, lots of luck in your new career."

"What do you mean?"

"I mean, what are you going to do when you get this CD? I just did a quick calculation on the back of an envelope, and there are, at most, 175,760 possible combinations of license plates beginning with '27' that could be issued by the state. That assumes that everything possible from '270' through '279' has been put on the street and that the state has moved on to issuing plates beginning with '280' and higher."

"How the hell do you get that?"

"Wait a minute . . . I need to check something. That number might be a little high."

Martelli could hear Missy tapping on her keyboard.

"Okay . . . here's what I was looking for. I wanted to make sure there were no exceptions that would impact my calculation. In fact, there are. In Iowa, the assignment of plates for automobiles began with '001 AAA' and continued to the present, though it will exclude '000 SAA' through '999 SHG' as well as the 'U' series and 'V' series.[25]

"So, the number I gave you is high. Let's forget for a moment the entire 'S' series as well as the 'U' and 'V' series. So, take 23 times 26 times 26 and you end up with 15,548 possible combinations for *each* initial three-numbered set. In all, there are ten sets in the '27' series, so just for starters, the state has issued 155,480 license plates beginning with '27'. To that, you still have to add the portion of the 'S' series that's not excluded by their assignment policy."

---

25 http://en.wikipedia.org/wiki/Vehicle_registration_plates_of_Iowa

"S#$%, Missy. I call you to get *good* news!"

"Well, Martelli, the good news is, the state of Iowa won't run out of license plate numbers for quite some time.

"But look . . . send me the CD when you get it. Then, if you even *suspect* someone, get the last number or even one of the letters on the plate, I'll get you the names associated with plates of interest. The CD still may turn out to be a good thing to have."

"Thanks, Missy!

"Oh, yes . . . one last thing. Jamar had a sketch artist sit down with the DC patrolman who stopped the perp and grab his likeness. I have the sketch, so at least we can broadcast that piece of information to State and local police authorities. Maybe we'll hope get lucky and someone will spot the guy.

"You certainly can use a break, Lou!"

Thirteen

'*H*ello, this is Detective Lou Martelli. I'm with the New York Police Department. Is Mrs. Selma Holtzmann home? I'd like to take just a few minutes of her time to talk about her experience with Berranger Biotechnology Systems."

"Mrs. Holtzmann is my mother. She's not well, sir. I'm afraid she won't be able to come to the phone. Is there something that I can help you with? I'm her son, Terrell."

"Terrell—and please call me Lou, if you would—know, first, how sorry I was to hear about your mother. I'm somewhat familiar with her condition as a result of an investigation I'm conducting that is related to a matter pertaining to Berranger Biotech and their drug, *HerDeciMax*."

"Detective—I'm sorry... Lou—that drug worked miracles for my mother. She has HER2-positive breast cancer. I don't know if you're familiar with the disease, but it's very aggressive and has a high risk of recurrence. We were fortunate that my mother's doctor, Doc Ewing, was able to get her into the Phase III trial of Berranger's drug, something that was possible only because of her condition at the time. It was touch and go, though, for a while . . . we didn't know if Berranger was even going to be able to include the hospital in Des Moines in their trial."

"What do you mean?"

"Well, as best I could understand from talking to Doc Ewing, Berranger was running low on money and needed to raise additional capital. But Doc said that the price of the stock kept getting driven down day after day, even though the general market was holding steady. I read that in the Des Moines paper . . . in an article my step-sister, Millie Fergesen, wrote. She's on the staff of the *Plains Courier,* you know."

Lou jotted down a note to contact Millie Fergesen.

"I asked Doc Ewing why this was happening, and he said he didn't know. But his fear was that if Berranger wasn't successful in raising a significant amount of money by selling stock on the open market or by doing a private placement, they would have to cut back on the number of participants they could enroll in the Phase III trial. That, in turn, he said, would impact the ability of the company to demonstrate that the drug worked because Berranger wouldn't be able to get enough data to do the statistics required in the time they had allocated to the trial."

"I see." *I need to look into this,* Martelli thought. *Sounds like more manipulation, to me.* "But, apparently, Berranger was able to raise the money, right?"

"Praise the Lord, yes. Mom had run out of options. *HerDeciMax* was her last hope. If Berranger hadn't opened a trial center in Des Moines, my mother would have died years ago . . . a horrible, slow, painful death.

"Even so, there was no assurance that she would get Berranger's drug because, as you may know, when drug companies run trials of this type, the people who participate in them don't know whether they will be given a placebo or the drug that is being tested. Basically, these tests are, what did Doc call them? Oh, yeah, I memorized it . . . 'large, randomized, double blind, placebo-controlled studies'.[26] Boy, ain't that a mouthful? But when you live with someone who is fighting cancer, you need to learn an awful lot, and you need to learn it *fast* if you're going to help them."

"Randomized, double blind, and placebo-controlled studies?"

"Well, each person is randomly assigned to receive either the drug or a placebo. The people in the trials don't know which treatment they receive. And the use of a placebo—that is, the fake treatment—allows the docs to isolate the effect of the actual drug."

"I get it, Terrell. Sounds like these studies could take quite a while."

"Oh, yeah . . . years, considering the administration of the drug, the collection of the data, the analysis, and so forth. Fortunately, *HerDeciMax* is what they call a 'small molecule', so it came in a pill. Mother was given a month's supply of whatever she was to take . . . placebo or drug. Then, I would drive her to Des Moines once a month for a physical examination by one of Berranger's physicians. Even she didn't know who was getting the placebo or *HerDeciMax*."

"That must have been some trip each month, Terrell."

"Naw, it wasn't too bad. Our farm is just north of Guthrie Center, up around the intersection of County Road N70 and 215th Street, so I would just catch State Route 44 East in town and head on over to Route 415, before heading south into Des Moines. It wasn't difficult. Took about 45 to 50 minutes each way."

26 http://en.wikipedia.org/wiki/Clinical_trial

"And what happened?"

"Well, I'll tell you, Lou, it was amazing. For a few months, we didn't see anything. But then, slowly, mother began to feel better. And even the doctors were amazed. They said that her cancer appeared to be going into remission. They couldn't be sure, of course, that it was due to the drug—they didn't know who was getting the real thing or a placebo—but there was no other explanation for what they were observing."

"She must have been elated."

"*We* were elated! We were beside ourselves with joy. Lou, she got her life back. One morning, I found her out in the barn at 5 AM, running the milking machines. She hadn't done that in two years. It was the miracle we had been praying for in church every Sunday for the last five years. I'll tell you this, but for God's sake, don't tell my mother, I broke down and cried. I had to go back to the house. I couldn't stop crying for ten minutes. Finally, I went out to the barn and helped her with some of the other chores."

"I only can imagine how you felt, Terrell."

"And then, one day, about two or three years ago, we received word from the founder and president of Berranger—Dr. Smithson, as I recall. . .he's a real gentleman—that they had 'unblinded' the Phase III trial and mother had indeed been given his company's drug. He said that a special meeting had been called by the FDA in Washington, DC—I think he called it an *advisory committee* or something like that—to consider whether or not to approve the drug for general use. He wondered if mother felt well enough to travel to Washington and appear at the meeting.

"Well, mother was most agreeable to appearing, but she was too proud to accept the money offered to her by Dr. Smithson.

She said she would have her son—me—drive her out, and all he had to do was tell her when and where to appear. She said she would be happy to tell her story to anyone who would listen. Dr. Smithson said he would send her all the particulars as well as some guidance as to what she might want to say and how long she could speak."

"So, you drove her to Washington?"

"Oh, yeah. We couldn't afford to fly. We have a little farm out here, not much in the way of savings, and things haven't been going that well over the last eight years since mother lost her second husband. So, mother and I just piled into my car—"

"Your car?"

"Yep, just an old tan, 1989 Pontiac, Lou. Nothing special. Pretty beat up, that's for sure, but it's all we got for transportation other than the old Ford F-150 we use on the farm. Oh, yes, and our old John Deere tractor, of course. Mother asked some of the neighbors to take care of the livestock, and we took off for Washington, stopping at night at the cheapest motels we could find. It wasn't the most pleasant trip, from the standpoint of accommodations. But I'll tell you, Lou . . . having that time with my mother was something I wouldn't trade for *anything* on Earth.

"Anyway, we got to Washington, and showed up at the meeting, just as planned. Had to sit through a lot of medical mumbo-jumbo, but that was to be expected. Finally, in the afternoon, they asked some patients to speak. Mother was one of them. I thought she did well. However, three of the people on the panel dozed off while she was talking, and it unnerved her a little. She stumbled in one or two places, and I saw her staring at them. I knew she was hurt. I mean, how would you feel, coming all that distance, telling how this drug had put your cancer in remission, and then seeing these people paying no attention to what you were saying. I wanted to go up to each of them and shake them by their shoulders."

"I understand you said a few things in the meeting that didn't exactly sit well with the chairperson."

"Well, what would you do, Lou, if *your* mother was dying and had come all that way, at her own expense, to tell people about the drug that had saved her, only to have them pay her no mind? I was really angry, and I told those people so. They asked me to leave the meeting, and I did. And I apologized, later. But there was no excuse for the way those people behaved. That was totally inconsiderate of them!"

"I certainly can understand that, Terrell."

"And then, to top it off, one of the people who dozed off, I'm told, voted against approval of the drug. Dr. Smithson also told me a while back that this same person had written some kind of article, I don't know what it was, saying bad things about *HerDeciMax*. In any event, the drug wasn't approved, and the FDA told Dr. Smithson he needed to go back and run some more tests. That's a cryin' shame. Lots of women probably died because they couldn't get his company's drug. I can feel my blood boil every time I think about it . . . and I *do* think about it. Often!"

"I understand, Terrell. It must be very difficult for you to look back and think about how all of this happened. But at least your mother's cancer went into remission and she had several good years that otherwise would have been denied her."

"That's true, Lou, and for that we are thankful. But now, the cancer has metastasized, even though Berranger has provided her with their drug free of charge all this time. There's nothing more we can do. I feel totally helpless.

"I've arranged for hospice in our farmhouse because mother insists that she will die in the same house where she was born. I'd be the last person on Earth to deny her that wish. But she doesn't have long, Lou. We're just going day to day now."

"So, you basically have been out there, on the farm, full time for the last several weeks, is that correct, Terrell?"

"Yes, of course. I'm the only one here looking after mother, other than the good people providing hospice care. Why do you ask?"

"Just curious. By the way, for the record, do you happen to remember the first three digits of the license plate on your Pontiac? I'm trying to tie up some loose ends out here, and having the information sure would help."

"Sure . . . let me think for a minute . . . the car plates are different from the truck plates, but still, I need to sort them out in my mind. Oh, yes . . . now I remember. The numbers on the car plates are '297'. The plates are issued for Guthrie County. Does that help you?"

"That's a big help, Terrell. Thanks.

"Look, I've taken up way too much of your time. You have been most helpful. I'm truly sorry about your mother. I wish there were something I could say or do that would help. Just know that you both are in my prayers."

"Thanks, Lou. That means a lot. I'll tell mother."

"Take care, Terrell."

Terrell hung up the phone and found himself shaking . . . shaking with rage as he thought about his conversation with Martelli and his beloved mother's terrible ordeal with breast cancer.

Fourteen

'A lexa Lindsay Beauvais! Light of my life! Thanks for stopping by. Something's been bothering me ever since I spoke with Mrs. Holtzmann's son. Remember. . . he was the one who was escorted from the meeting after yelling at three of the panel's members who fell asleep during his mother's presentation in support of Berranger's drug."

"Oh, yes. I read the entire transcript, Lou. That was a real nice display of respect from the Advisory Committee panel, wasn't it? *Not!*"

Lou laughed. "You sound like my 16-year-old daughter!"

"That's because I'm only six years older than her, Lou, or haven't you noticed?" She winked at him.

"You said something was bothering you, Lou. How can I help?"

"Talk to me about PIPEs."

"Pipes? You mean, like, the kind you put tobacco in?"

"No, I'm talking about 'Private Investment in Public Equity'. When I was talking with Terrell Holtzmann, he mentioned that Berranger's stock had been driven so low in value during the early stages of the Phase III trial for *HerDeciMax* that the company almost didn't have enough cash to open a trial center in Des Moines. And Terrell said that based on what Mrs. Holtzmann's doctor said and what Terrell had read in the Des Moines paper, this was at a time when the general market was relatively stable.

"I smelled a rat, so I started digging into all the information I could find in John Williamson's files . . . his e-mails, inter-office memoranda, letters . . . every scrap of paper, even those yellow Post-It notes that seem to be everywhere. Can you believe it, he seems to have kept notes on them, and then, he would paste the notes on regular desktop printer paper and put them in his files. The guy was really obsessive-compulsive about keeping everything . . . for which I will be eternally grateful!

"In any event, I found a yellow sticky with a notation to the effect 'Call Charles re getting KR to run stories on his blog about Berranger running out of money and how they may be forced to do a PIPE. That should drop price at least $2 or more.' There was no date on the sticky, but just looking at where it was inserted in the file indicated that it would have been written about the time that Berranger was attempting to raise additional funds for the *HerDeciMax* trial. There also was another note, on the same piece of printer paper, on which he—at least I have to believe that it was Williamson—scribbled 'Call PW at JDB and have them call Berranger, offering to do a PIPE. After call is made, have KR run rumor on blog that JDB in discussions with Berranger to do a PIPE. That should be good for another point on the downside.'"

Alexa nodded. "It all makes perfect sense. And now, I understand even better why someone would want to kill Mr. John Williamson. There he was trying to sink Berranger, without one thought given to the people whose lives depend on obtaining the drug!"

"I agree. . . from the context of those notes, I gather that for a company to raise money using PIPEs is about as welcome as having your appendix removed without anesthesia."

"Worse, Lou, because with PIPEs, the patient may not survive. Look, PIPEs are complicated. A traditional PIPE is one in which stock, either common or preferred, is issued at a set price to raise capital for the issuer. A structured PIPE, on the other hand, issues convertible debt—common or preferred shares.[27] Don't try to understand these terms. Just know that depending on the toxic terms of the transaction, a PIPE may dilute existing shareholders' equity ownership. And certain PIPE investments that were executed in the past—primarily those involving hedge-funds—violated US government security laws. Here, the problem largely centered on hedge funds that used PIPE securities to 'cover' shares that the funds had *shorted* in anticipation of the PIPE offering. In some of these instances, the SEC—and I'll have to give them credit here—was able to demonstrate that the funds knew about the upcoming PIPE offering in which they would be involved, for God's sake, *prior to shorting shares.*"[28] [29]

"Ah ha! You're going soft on the SEC, Lex."

"The hell I am! Consider the case of Gary Aguirre, the former SEC staff attorney and Senior Counsel who was fired in 2005 for aggressively pursuing an investigation of suspected insider trading involving one of the nation's largest hedge funds, Pequot Capital Management (PCM). He was asked to submit testimony

27 http://www.investopedia.com/terms/p/pipe.asp
28 http://en.wikipedia.org/wiki/Private_investment_in_public_equity
29 http://www.sec.gov/litigation/litreleases/lr19607.htm

to the United States Senate Committee on the Judiciary pertaining to the Commission's lax enforcement of the nation's security laws. In the matter of hedge funds that engage in insider trading, Aguirre rhetorically asked during his testimony how the SEC was doing. His answer: the SEC—aside from cases involving PIPEs—had brought only three cases against hedge funds for insider trading and recovered a total of $110,000.[30] Does that sound like your and my tax dollars at work? And remember...this was while the illustrious Mr. Bernie Madoff was romping and stomping all over Wall Street!"

Lou put his arms straight up into the air. "Okay, okay. I surrender! I surrender!

"So, Lex, even the rumor that Berranger *might* be talking to a hedge fund or some other source of equity about doing a PIPE would be enough to suggest, at the least, that the company's outstanding shares would be diluted. And that would send the so-called 'smart money' stampeding for the door. Sell on the rumor, right? That's what the Street must have done. It sold Berranger's stock...probably sold it 'short' by the ton in an attempt to drive the company into the ground."

"That's exactly what happened. Rent the movie <u>Wall Street</u>, Lou. The main character, Gordon Gekko, had this to say about that. *'It's all about bucks, kid. The rest is conversation.'* You're looking at a real-live example in this case. Doesn't it just make you proud of our financial markets and the people at the helm?"

"Frankly, Lex, I've come to the conclusion that it's those people—the people *at the helm*, as you say—who are taking the <u>greatest country</u> in the world straight into the ground!"

30 http://judiciary.senate.gov/hearings/testimony.cfm?id=2437&wit_id=5485

Fifteen

'Guthrie County Constable's Office, Officer Lake, speaking. Please hold. . . . I'm sorry, this is Officer Lake. How may I direct your call?"

"Officer Lake, this is Homicide Detective Lou Martelli of the New York Police Department. Is Constable Hutchinson in?"

"Yes, sir. I'll let him know that you are on the line."

"Good afternoon, Detective Martelli. This is Constable Hutchinson. We don't get too many calls from people back East, so I suspect you're not calling to exchange the pleasantries of the day."

"No, sir, I'm afraid this is more in the line of duty. And please, call me Lou, if you would."

"Pleased to meet you, Lou. My friends call me Brad."

"Okay, Brad. No, this call is definitely about business. I need your help solving two homicides, one that occurred recently in Manhattan and the other, in Washington, DC. Both had the same MO. Perhaps you've read about them. The perpetrator, whoever he may be, severed his victims' heads and left them on prominent statues in the two cities. The bodies haven't been found. What we *do* know is that whoever is doing this is pretty skilled with butcher knives—perhaps he works in a butcher shop, in a meat market, or on a farm—and he drives an older car, probably a domestic make, with what we believe to be Iowa plates beginning with the numbers '2' and '7', in that order. The common thread between the two murders seems to be a drug company by the name of Berranger Biotechnology Systems, which makes a drug called *HerDeciMax*."

"I've heard of that drug."

"Well, you probably heard of it in connection with one of your county's residents, Mrs. Selma Holtzmann."

"Yes! Of course! Selma was dying of breast cancer . . . terrible disease. Fortunately, Doc Ewing got her into a drug trial at the hospital in Des Moines. They were testing a new drug produced by Berranger. It *was HerDeciMax*, all right. They told her there were no guarantees that she even would be given the drug. She could have gotten a placebo.

"If that had been the case, as I understand it, she most likely would have died within two or three months. But she said she had nothing to lose, and they put her into the trial. Well, you must know the story."

"Oh, yes . . . I just got off the phone with her son, Terrell. He told me it was a miracle. Even though no one knew who got the drug during the trial, it was just a matter of time before the doctors, and Selma herself, were pretty sure she was in the arm of the study that was receiving Berranger's new treatment."

"Lou, it was a miracle. I saw her at a town hall meeting just before she started taking the drug, and it almost made me cry. We're old Guthrie Center High School alumni—Class of 1977—and boy, seeing her that way, knowing what a bundle of energy she had been in school, made me feel so helpless . . . and angry. Why her, I kept asking myself? Why her? She's a good, decent person."

"I don't think anyone has the answer to that question, Brad."

Neither man spoke for a moment. Then, Brad continued.

"Married her old high school sweetheart, she did. . .Everett Holtzmann, captain of the *Tigers'* football team. He led them to two State Championships in 1975 and 1976. They were the homecoming king and queen. . .the envy of everyone in the school. They bought a farm after graduation with what they saved during their high school years. Selma worked behind the soda fountain at the old drug store on State Street while Everett worked on his dad's farm as a paid 'hand'. Once they had their own place, they worked hard together to make a 'go' of it. Held off having children until the farm was up and running. Terrell came along in the early 1980's."

"Sounds like things were going pretty well for them."

"Well, they were, until the winter of 1994, when Everett's tractor tipped over on top of him while he was clearing snow from their driveway. He was pushing the snow towards the side of the road, and the right, front wheel of the tractor slid into the drainage ditch. He tried to jump clear, but the tractor rolled over on him. He died a horrible death. Selma tried to carry on without Everett, but it was difficult. She almost lost the farm once to the bank.

"A few years later, she met Karl Fergesen. Karl had lost his wife two years earlier due to ovarian cancer. The Fergesens were a wonderful couple, Lou. The salt of the earth. For years, Karl and his first wife took in foster children, both boys *and* girls. Now—"

"Wait. . .did you say they had other children living with them over the years?"

125

"Oh, yes...a whole string of them...perhaps a dozen or more. Truth be told, the Fergesens needed additional help around their farm. They had a daughter, Millie...smart as a whip, she was. But she couldn't handle the really tough chores. Karl needed men to help him with the livestock and the crops. From time to time, his wife asked for help in the kitchen and around the house, so they would bring in a girl. That way, too, Millie had someone to play with. Some of those kids were pretty sharp, Lou. Had good heads on their shoulders.

"The Fergesens worked with the State through the Guthrie County Foster Care Agency. Some kids stayed with them only a few months...those were the ones that didn't fit into life on a farm or just plain caused problems. It isn't easy, as you can imagine, getting up at 5 AM on a winter morning and having to go out to the barn and hook up the milking machines. Quite a few stuck it out, though, because the Fergesens treated them as if they were their own kin. Frankly, some of the kids thought of them as second parents. You can imagine the home life those kids must have come from."

"Yeah, Brad, it's a shame what some kids go through. So, what happened?"

"Well, sir, things started to go downhill fast when Gertrude— that was Karl's wife's name—took sick with ovarian cancer. Because of the hospital expenses—they had no insurance—it was just a matter of time before they were drowning in debt. The bank held off foreclosing until shortly after Gertrude died sometime in 1994, but then, they took the farm. There was nothing anyone could do. Karl worked odd jobs on several farms in the area, but it wasn't long before he was spending more and more time at the Holtzmann farm. Eventually, he and

Selma married in May or June, 1996. Hell, I can't remember. I guess you could say it was a marriage of convenience.

"Regardless, the Holtzmann farm was too much for just two people to manage—Terrell wasn't that old, at that point, maybe 13 or 14 or so—so Karl and Selma brought foster children in to help them as well."

"Do you remember any of their names, Brad?"

"Hell, Lou. Do you know how bad my memory is? I suggest you check with the State's foster care agency. I'm not sure what they can and can't release to you, but perhaps your police department has ways of getting such information."

"I'll look into it, Brad. Thanks. Please, go on."

"Well, things seemed to be going along pretty well until Karl came down with lung cancer—the man smoked three packs a day of those little black cigars, can you believe it? Let's see . . . that was in late 1999."

"I guess an addiction like that is hard to kick."

"Isn't that the truth? Well, sir, Selma continued to work the farm with Terrell and, at the same time, nurse Karl the best she could, but it was rough. Karl died in January, 2002 . . . in the middle of winter. Now, here's one thing I will *never* forget—"

"What's that, Brad?"

"The day we buried old Karl. The temperature was minus 20 degrees Fahrenheit and the wind was blowing 30 miles per hour. The backhoe broke a tooth trying to dig his grave. We weren't sure we'd be able to bury him when we did. Some thought we'd have to wait until spring.

"When it was over, Selma and Terrell just picked up and kept going, with the help of some foster kids. Those kids loved her. There wasn't anything they wouldn't do for her."

"Any names, Brad?"

"Again, Lou, I think it would be best to contact the State. Besides, there could be real privacy issues here, and I don't want to get involved in those, especially in this day and age. The last thing I need is some lawyer getting on my back, especially with me up for re-election in the fall. But I'll tell you this...some of the kids were smart as a whip. One, Selma used to tell me, would study early in the morning before setting up the milking machines and again, late at night, before going to sleep. He loved books, and was constantly begging Terrell to bring him stuff from the library when Terrell went to town for supplies. Selma loved that kid as if he was her own, and the kid loved her. But damned if I can remember his name. He was a tall boy, that I do remember. Never caused any problems. Church goin', too. Very religious."

"I understand, Brad. And you're absolutely correct. Any inquiry has to be done through legal channels, with care taken to protect the privacy of the individuals involved." Lou was busy scribbling as he talked, punctuating his notes regarding investigations into the identities of Karl's and Selma's foster children with exclamation point after exclamation point.

"So, when did Selma come down sick?"

"Let's see...I think it was early in 2004 when she was diagnosed with breast cancer. Maybe March or April, right after the last of the snow melted. Certainly before anyone put seed into the ground. Could have been the stress and all...I don't know. They tried chemo, and it slowed the cancer down a bit. But still, it seemed clear that the disease couldn't be stopped.

"The lady certainly deserved better, that's for sure, Lou."

Martelli waited a moment before speaking. "And that's when her doctor got her into the trial?"

"I think he got her into the trial sometime in 2006, if my memory serves me correctly. But you know what? Millie Fergesen, her step-daughter who works for the *Plains Courier* in Des Moines, wrote the whole story up for the newspaper, beginning when her mother first found out she had breast cancer.

"Millie did a whole series of articles that followed her mother through her initial diagnosis, the radiation treatments, problems her doctor had in getting her into the *HerDeciMax* trial, Berranger's trouble raising money, and the people on Wall Street who were behind attempts to put Berranger out of business.

"You should talk to her about what she uncovered. Maybe there's something in the articles she wrote that will provide some leads for you. I'll see if I can find the articles and send them to you. Come to think of it, it probably would be better to get everything directly from her. I highly recommend you call her!"

"That's good advice, Brad. I'll be sure to give her a call. If what you say is true, and I have no doubt that it is, she probably *is* the best source of information on the problems Berranger encountered in attempting to bring their drug to market."

"No question about it. She even wrote a detailed description of what happened at the *HerDeciMax* Advisory Committee meeting in Washington two years ago. I think her newspaper flew her out so she could attend. Boy, that was something. You heard about that, didn't you?"

"Oh, yes. That was the one where, as I understand it, Terrell was ejected from the meeting for yelling at some of the doctors on the *HerDeciMax* Advisory Committee panel."

"Look, Lou, he's a good kid. Never gave his mother a lick of trouble. Worked side by side with her through all kinds of weather, troubles with the bank, and the loss of two husbands. He never once complained. The boy even found time to become a volunteer fireman. Saved a little girl one time, he did, by rushing into a burning barn after she had set it afire while playing with matches. If it weren't for him, she would have died and the barn would have burned to the ground with the loss of twelve head of cattle.

"I don't blame him for getting angry, considering how those people didn't have the decency even to listen to what his mother had to say. And then, for the damn fools in Washington to refuse to approve the drug after it was proven to have worked so well for her . . . well, I smell a rat. Frankly, we in the Midwest would sooner sleep with a rattlesnake as trust a Washington bureaucrat. The whole lot of them aren't worth a warm cup of spit!"

"Well, Brad, I try to stay as far away from Washington as possible, for any number of reasons. And yes, my gut tells me that Terrell *is* a good kid. I could sense that in his voice. Seems totally dedicated to his mom. I guess he's been sticking pretty close to the farm these past several weeks, right?"

"Absolutely. Except for doing chores around the farm and coming to town for supplies, he hasn't left her side, best I can tell.

"I don't think Selma has much time left, Lou. Terrell's brought hospice in for her. At least that gives him time to tend to the farm during the day. But at night, he's the only one available to provide care for his mother. I was out to their place two or three times in the last two weeks to bring them groceries and other supplies. Terrell was hard at work on both occasions. There's no way he can get away from the place for more then a few hours at a time, and that's just during the day, to tend to business in town. Any particular reason for asking?"

"No, just checking all the boxes, Brad. Well, thanks for your time. I'll give Millie a call. Sounds like she might be able to help me tie up some loose ends."

"I suspect she might, Lou. And ask her to tell you about that story she did two years ago . . . the one that almost got her killed! Man, that was a close call. But she got the story, *and* the 'Pinnacle Award for Excellence in Investigative Journalism'. That gal ain't afraid of anyone when it comes to going after a story."

"Sounds like my kind of woman, Brad."

Brad laughed. "Just be careful, Lou. She'll pick you clean, and you won't even know it happened!"

"Thanks for the warning. By the way, I'll fax your office the sketch of the man who was stopped by a DC patrolman just before the head of their victim was found on the statue in downtown Washington. If it should look familiar, please give me a call."

"Will do, Lou."

"Thanks, Brad. Be well."

Lou tapped the 'hook' on his phone's console, and dialed his department's office. "Hey, Joannie, baby, it's Martelli!"

"Don't you 'Joannie, baby' me, Detective Louis Martelli! It means you want something."

"Moi?"

"Yes, you! In French or any other language."

"Okay, okay . . . did my CD from Iowa come in yet?"

"No, Lou. Some clerk upstairs forgot to journal an entry in the accounting system last week, and I just caught it. The check was never 'cut'.

"But I have everything straightened out now. I'm going to send the request for the dump of the license plate registration data and our check to the Iowa State capital in this afternoon's FedEx. When I spoke to the clerk in Des Moines, she suggested that I use their 'Expedited Service'. So, I added the $200 necessary to turn our request around in 24 hours. The clerk, Mrs. Morrison, said she personally would ensure our request was taken care of the moment it arrived. I put it to her attention."

"Thanks, Joannie. What would I do without you?"

"I don't want to find out, Lou! I don't like the implications."

"Oh...oh...one more thing."

"You only get one request today, Martelli!"

"I know...I owe you, Joanie. But have you ever attempted to obtain information related to the names of foster children from any State agency? Ever?"

"Can't be done through this office, Lou. That's something you'll have to go through the courts to get. The privacy laws are so strict these days that it's impossible to learn anything about kids who are in, or who have been in, the foster care system, regardless of who and where they are. The best thing for you to do is talk to the District Attorney's office. But without probable cause and hard evidence, I doubt you'll even be able to convince them to take your request to a judge."

"Thanks, Joanie. As always, I appreciate your advice...and help! Take care."

"Take care, Lou. And good luck."

Sixteen

'*T*his is the *Plains Courier,* your Number One newspaper in Des Moines. Please hold." Lou looked at his watch. It was mid-afternoon in New York, so he hoped his chances were good that he might catch Millie Fergesen coming back from a late lunch.

"I'm sorry, how may I direct your call?"

"This is Detective Lou Martelli, Manhattan Homicide. Is—"

"Is that Manhattan, Kansas, or Manhattan, New York, Detective?"

"Ah, New York, ma'am...New York City, to be exact. I wonder if you would be so kind as to put me through to Ms. Millie Fergesen."

"Transferring!"

The phone rang three times. *Dammit,* thought Lou. He was about to give up when her heard the line open.

"Fergesen!" Millie Fergesen was all business. A 2003 graduate of the University of Iowa with a BA in Journalism, she graduated *cum laude* and immediately joined the *Plains Courier,* where she had worked her way through college as a 'stringer' and intern. At 5 feet, 2 inches and 105 pounds, she maintained a pace that left people 10 years younger breathless.

She was all about form over style, as evidenced by her short black hair—"What's your problem? It dries fast in the morning!"—and work attire—"What's wrong with blue jeans, a chambray shirt, and insulated vest? I can be out of the office, into my car, and on my way in 2 minutes, regardless of how cold it is!"

Millie's life was guided by two tenets: (1) Life in the United States must be based on the 'Rule of Law', and (2) Governments at all levels—Federal, State, and local—have an obligation to protect and defend the rights of individuals *at all costs!* Violate either or both of Millie's tenets, and bad things happened. More than one felon formerly of the greater Des Moines area, but now a guest of the State of Iowa prison system, learned too late that in Millie's hands, a computer keyboard became a 'weapon of mass destruction'. . .*his destruction!*

"Ms. Fergesen, this is Detective Lou Martelli, New York City Police Department. I was just on the phone with Constable Brad Hutchinson in Guthrie Center regarding a murder investigation I'm pursuing. It's tied, in some respects, to something that you've been writing about. Frankly, he almost *insisted* I touch base with you."

"Oh, is that so. What's the subject, Detective?"

"Please call me 'Lou'. May I call you 'Millie'?"

"Sure. . .believe me, I've been called worse. So, it's your nickel! Are you just calling to chat about the weather, which isn't that bad now that it's March, or are you fishing for something?"

Lou was startled by her directness. He'd been confronted by plenty of pushy reporters in New York City. This kind of abruptness was *de rigueur* for that crowd. But he hardly expected to hear the lack of civility he was hearing from a reporter in the Midwest, and a young woman at that.

"Well, Millie, the subject is Berranger's drug *HerDeciMax*."

"Ah, yes. And just how does that figure into your murder investigation, Lou?"

Lou could hear Millie tapping on her keyboard. He suddenly realized that Millie was about to feel around in the 'pockets' of his mind, looking for anything she could use. *I need to slow this down before she coerces me into doing a memory dump!*

"Before we begin, Brad told me to make sure I congratulated you on winning a prestigious journalism award two years ago."

"You mean the 'Pinnacle Award for Excellence in Investigative Journalism'? Hell, that and 25 cents will get you into a pay toilet."

"He said you almost lost your life putting that story together. Had one of those 'near-death' experiences, did you?"

"Oh, yeah. And a real thrill it was, too! Ever had one, Lou?"

"Oh, nothing like yours, I'm sure. Just the usual daily battles with our famous New York taxi drivers."

Millie laughed. "Well, here's a tip. The key to surviving near-death experiences is in the execution. Unless you do it correctly, they tend to be non-habit-forming."

"Keep going, Millie. I'm taking notes on this."

"Lou, you are so full of bulls#$%!"

"I know, but I couldn't help myself. Go on. I really do want to hear what happened."

"Well, I got a tip about three years ago that a major crime syndicate had opened for business in Des Moines. . . prostitution, gambling, racketeering, and. . . murder-for-hire. I started snooping around. . . you know, talking to my informants on the street, looking at real estate records, checking with the guys who run the pawn shops, and the like. Then I started to connect the dots. Pretty soon, weird things started to happen. I got strange phone calls in the middle of the night, but there would be no one on the other end. After two of those, I had the line tapped by the phone company, but the police found they came from pay phones. Then I'd see cars following me at various times during the day and night. Once, they tried to run me off the road around midnight...down near Milo, in Warren County. I was coming home from visiting my uncle. They even threatened my grandmother, so I had to ask the police to protect her. Meanwhile, I kept digging. It took about eight months before everything started to come together."

"Sounds like you made good progress."

"Too good! In the ninth month after I began my investigation, Mr. Big invited me to meet with him at his office downtown. Said he and I needed to talk. I told my boss where I was going, gave him a manila folder containing my story and all my evidence, jumped into my car, which had been in the newspaper's parking lot since 4 AM that day, and drove to Mr. Big's bar in the seedy part of town. There was a parking lot located next to Mr. Big's building, and as it happened, I parked right outside his office, though I didn't know it at the time. The building was one of those three-story brick-façade jobs with a bar on the first floor and apartments above...built in the 1920's. The area's loaded with 'em. The sides are covered with faded advertisements that were painted on them in the 1940's and 1950's."

"Yeah, I know what you mean. We have them here as well, in certain neighborhoods."

"Well, anyway, I was early. So I walked across the street to grab a cup of coffee. No sooner had I stepped into the donut shop when there was a flash of light and a thunderous explosion that lifted everything in the shop a foot off the floor. I hit the deck, and when the dust and glass settled, I got up, looked at the parking lot, and all I saw was a mass of twisted, burned-out vehicles, one on top of another! Lou, those assholes must have rigged my car with a bomb. But somehow, it didn't go off when it was supposed to. Instead, it took out Mr. Big's bar and just about everyone in it within 30 feet of where I had it parked. They never found Mr. Big or his lieutenants. Which as far as I'm concerned, as a taxpayer, is fine. The paper published my story the next day, and the publisher nominated me for the Pinnacle Award the following week."

"Damn! That was close!"

"I'll say. The next thing I knew, the State moved in and took over the case. Within six months, they had everyone who was still alive and involved in the syndicate behind bars. But you know what really pissed me off?"

"That the State put a clamp on the news once they took over the case?"

"Hell, no! What really got my blood pressure up was my damn automobile insurance company. Those jerks would only give me the Blue Book value on the car. Give me a freakin' break! Lou, that Chevy only had 102,000 miles on it! It was barely broken in!"

"A 'cherry', Millie!"

"Damn straight. I'll tell you this. When I get done with my next story, I'm going to look into the entire automobile insurance industry. It's time someone tore them a new one!

"Now, where the hell were we? Oh, yeah...how does Berranger's drug *HerDeciMax* figure into your murder investigation?"

"Okay.... here's the deal. You and I are going to have this conversation off the record. You must promise me that anything we discuss will *not* find its way into print, no way, no how...until this case is solved. Even more to the point, this call never took place!"

"So, what's in it for me?"

"All I can promise you, Millie, is that if and when the case breaks wide open, I will give you a running head start on the competition. And believe me, the story will be a big one! From a career standpoint, it could push you right through the glass ceiling!"

"Okay...you have my interest. What do you want to know?"

"Well, to begin—

"Whoops...hold on...cellphone...yes...Millie, can I call you back in 5 minutes? I have my wife on the phone."

"Sure, Lou. I'll grab a cup of coffee in the meantime."

Seventeen

'Sorry about that, Millie. I had almost forgotten about the PTA meeting this evening. My wife called to remind me to be home early. I've been going 18 hours a day since the homicide to which I'm assigned occurred, and one day blends into the next. It's been crazy.

"In any event, as I was starting to say, let's talk about Berranger's drug *HerDeciMax* and how it figures into my murder investigation."

"Okay, Lou. I'm very familiar with the drug, as you know. It's the one Selma Holtzmann was on during the Phase III trial conducted by Berranger. It's still being provided to her, as I understand. I covered all of this in my series of articles. Do you need copies?"

"Yes, if you don't mind. I saw your e-mail address on your paper's masthead. Why don't I send you an e-mail, and then, you can reply and attach pdf copies of the articles. Would that be possible?"

"Sure. That's the best way to get you good copies for archival purposes. But you didn't call just to get my articles. You already went to the newspaper's Internet site, so you could have pulled the series down from there. Let's cut the foreplay, Lou, and 'get it on'. What do you *really* want?"

"Gee, Millie, do you talk to all the guys this way, or am I just special? Okay, okay . . . I'm going to play this hand with my cards 'face-up'."

Lou switched the phone from his right to his left hand and took his father's two silver dollars out of his right pants pocket. He started flipping one behind the other in the same way he flips chips at the poker tables in Vegas on family trips he, Steph, and the kids occasionally take during Easter Breaks in the school year.

"I'm holding the Ten, Jack, Queen, and King of *Spades*, and the 5 of *Hearts*."

♠10 ♠J ♠Q ♠K ♥5

"Bummer, Lou. One card short of a Royal Flush."

"Tell me about it. Here's how things stack up.

"The 10 of *Spades*. What I'm going to tell you, for the most part, here, can be found in the New York City and Washington, DC, newspapers. When I get into areas that are sensitive, I'll let you know, okay?"

"Okay . . . I understand."

"The 10 of *Spades* (♠10) represents the first murder. The vic was a Wall Street analyst named John Williamson who worked for the firm Bartlett, Cline, and Stephenson. He worked for a woman named Tricia Fournier, Executive Vice President and Manager, Equities Research. They had a campaign going for some time to keep the shares of Berranger under pressure."

"I uncovered that early in my investigation, Lou. All you had to do is watch the price action in the stock. It correlated almost one-for-one with the release of Williamson's and his partner's—"

"Jacobs'."

"Yeah, Williamson's and Jacobs' reports. Lou, there was another brokerage house that colluded with them. You'll find it mentioned in the second article in my series. The company was Parsons, Cline, and Mitchell. Both houses would release negative reports on the same day, like clockwork. You might want to keep an eye on the analysts over at the other brokerage house. They could be marked for death, as well."

"Okay, Millie. It might be worth going over to their offices and having a talk with them. By the way, with something that obvious, did anyone file a report with the SEC regarding the collusion that was uncovered?"

"Of course! Berranger shareholders were up in arms about it. I contacted several of them using private messages on the various Internet message boards. With one or two exceptions, the SEC just replied with their standard language. Wait a minute . . . let me grab one of the agency's e-mail responses . . . it's all government bull@#$%. Here it is:

"Thank you for your email and for taking the time to alert us to your concerns.

"We will carefully consider your request for an investigation. But at this point, our office can do nothing further to help you. This is because the SEC generally conducts its investigations

> on a confidential basis and neither
> confirms nor denies the existence of an
> investigation until we bring charges
> against someone involved. We cannot
> provide you with updates on the status
> of your complaint or of any pending
> SEC investigation. We know this policy
> can be frustrating, but it protects
> the integrity and effectiveness of our
> investigative process and preserves
> the privacy of the individuals and
> entities involved. Our policy is more
> fully described below.
>
> "Once again, thank you for writing to
> us."

"And, of course, they did nothing, Lou. This went on for two years. Again, your tax money at work! I guess they had more important things to do, like running Mr. Madoff to ground."

"Oh, yeah. . . that went really well, as I recall."

"One of the agency's finest hours!"

"One thing we never released to the press, and I want to remind you again on your promise not to release anything until we catch the murderer, at which time it will become known anyway, is that the first two numbers of the license plate of the car that was used to deliver the head to the site where it was found in the Financial District—which as you know was on the left horn of the Wall Street Bull statue—were '2' and '7'."

Lou could hear Millie typing furiously on her keyboard.

"And then we have the Jack of *Spades* (♠J). Murder Number 2, which took place in Washington, DC. This time the perp tossed the head into the lap of a statue in downtown Washington. The vic was none other than—"

"The illustrious Dr. Paul K. Broussard. I read it in *The Washington Post.* I saw Broussard in action at the *HerDeciMax* Advisory Committee meeting that took place in 2008, Lou. He was a real asshole. Not only did he denigrate the drug at every opportunity, but he fell asleep while the patients and patient advocates were pleading their cases. In the end, he voted NO on both questions.

"What I never could figure out was how in the world he *ever* was permitted to serve on the advisory committee in the first place. I know for a fact from other sources that he was in involved with BCaPharmaceutical on the trial of a drug that would compete with *HerDeciMax.* And yet, the FDA signed off on his waiver. I even obtained a copy of his waiver under the Freedom of Information Act. Lots of things were blacked out, but still, it looked like he had multiple conflicts of interest. Those pharmaceutical houses have figured out how to mask their involvement through CROs. But your mama didn't raise no dumb kids. . .you've already figured that out, right, Lou?"

"Oh, yeah. . .we have one smart lady on the staff who picked up on that in a heartbeat. But again, didn't people complain, if not to the SEC, then, perhaps, to Congress?"

"Sure, for all the good it did. One of the congressman in Iowa, I can't remember his name or district, wrote the House Committee on Energy and Commerce about the need for hearings. But in the end, the Committee bought the FDA's position that because a final decision had not yet been made regarding approval or non-approval of *HerDeciMax,* it would be premature to hold hearings."

"What? What does one thing have to do with the other? If there are irregularities in the vetting of personnel by the FDA for positions on advisory committees, what does that have to do with whether or not a drug has been approved?"

"I know, Lou. This is what passes for logic within the Beltway."

"By the way, the man we believe killed Williamson used the same car when he stopped to loop Broussard's head into the statue's lap. A DC patrolman pulled him over because of a burned-out headlight. Though the cop didn't do everything he should have done for a traffic 'stop', he was able to confirm for us the first two numbers on the rear license plate as '2' and '7' as well as to tell us that the car's plates were issued by Iowa."

"Now, this is getting *very* interesting, Lou!" Millie was typing like there was no tomorrow. You would have thought she had begun typing up her last story in the saga of Mrs. Selma Holtzmann and all she needed Lou to utter was the name of the murderer before typing '-30-' at the bottom and sending the article to her editor. *What does she know that I* need *to know?* thought Lou.

"Remember...this is off the record, Millie, and you promised not to release it! It's very sensitive. If my captain caught me giving you this information, I'd be in deep kimchi."

"Lou, you have my word. Ask anyone who knows me. I've *never* broken my word!"

"I believe you, Millie. Moving on to Queen of *Spades* (♠Q) I found information that leads me to believe that the man behind the plot to bring down Berranger may be the head of the firm that stands to lose the most if *HerDeciMax* becomes the new standard of care. He's Demetri Mihailov, MD, of

BCaPharmaceutical. Conversely, his company would retain its top spot in the treatment of breast cancer *if* he is successful in stopping Berranger *and* in bringing his company's new product to market in the next year."

"I mentioned BCaPharmaceutical as being Berranger's major competitor but couldn't cite Mihailov as the one who was attempting to 'take down' Berranger, Lou. I had information to that effect. However, our legal department insisted I provide them with evidence of Mihailov's involvement acquired from two *independent* sources before they would approve my story. When I couldn't come up with a second source, they killed the story. Where did you get your information?"

"My first hint came in the postscript to a memorandum from Fournier to Williamson, in which she referred to actions 'DM' was taking regarding someone with the initials 'PB'. It's not difficult to figure out who is being referenced here. I have tried to reach Mihailov and talk with him, perhaps even warn him to be careful. But every time I call, his secretary tells me he's tied up and will have to get back to me.

"It's clear he doesn't want to talk. Probably thinks I want to interrogate him about Williamson and Broussard, which, eventually, is something I will want to do. But first, I need to fit a few more of the pieces of this puzzle together. Meanwhile, his refusal to talk with me could cost him his life."

"Well, why not just summon him down to police headquarters in Manhattan or barge in on him at his office?"

"I thought of that. But I'm concerned about my being able to demonstrate 'probable cause' for dragging him down here or barging in on him. Besides, if I did drag him over here, knowing who he is, he'd probably show up with three lawyers in tow and refuse to say anything. It would be a waste of everyone's time, though it would give me the opportunity, of course, to warn him."

"Well, he'll have to suffer the consequences of his actions, Lou. Or is it 'inactions'? Regardless, he's a big boy."

"What's the story behind the fourth card, Lou?

"Ah, yes . . . the King of *Spades* (♠K). And here's where my gut is talking to me. Based on information I have from Constable Hutchinson, I'm beginning to think that my prime suspect is someone who has strong emotional ties to Selma . . . perhaps one of the foster kids that Karl and Selma brought into their home. It has to be someone who is pretty bright."

"Why do you say that?"

"Well, it would have taken a pretty intelligent person to kill the victims the way he did, drop the heads in areas where surveillance is second to none, dispose of the bodies, and disappear into the night, both in New York City and Washington, DC. Does that sound like anyone you know? Anyone resembling someone you might have interviewed for your series of articles?"

Millie said nothing. The line was completely silent. All of a sudden, Lou could hear her typing. Furiously.

"Millie? Did you hear my questions?"

"I heard you, Lou. Look, man, there are things I can say, and things I can't. Kids today may not value their privacy—hell, look at the pictures they post on the Internet of their sexploits or the sexting that goes on between highschoolers—but out here, among our older, more conservative population, we take privacy *very* seriously. I interviewed a lot of people in the course of writing up the series of articles on Selma Holtzmann. Most people wouldn't allow me to use their real names. Others only would give me permission to use their first names. The quotes I used in my articles were verified independently by my editor. That's how we got around problems related to quoting sources who insisted on anonymity.

"Now, I would be lying to you if I said no one was angry about how they viewed what was happening, both on Wall Street and within the FDA. People were *plenty* angry. Angry with Wall Street, angry with the FDA, angry with the SEC. Lots of them kept saying, 'That could be me instead of Selma!' Could they have committed murder because of their anger? I don't know. Who *really* knows what goes on in people's heads when emotions take over?

"In journalism, as you know, Lou, we protect our sources, no matter what! The confidentially of sources doctrine[31] for reporters is well recognized, and the consequences of violating it are significant and severe to *all* parties, society included. So, I'm sorry, Lou, I really can't comment on anything regarding the people I interviewed."

Lou took a deep breath. Instinctively, he knew Millie was correct. But something told him she knew who had committed the murders. He could not put his finger on it—it was a *hunch*—the kind of 'gut feeling' he had developed over the years and had come to trust. If he was correct, the murderer was one of the former foster children that Selma or, perhaps, Karl and Selma had brought into their home.

Now, it was a race against time. Could Lou find the killer before he struck again? Lou's thinking was that there would be one more murder. But what if he was wrong? What if there

---

31 Also known as the Reporter-Source Privilege

would be not only a third, but a fourth, and then fifth murder before he, Lou, caught a lucky break and the perpetrator of these heinous crimes was apprehended? One thing Lou knew for sure. Time was *not* on his side.

"I understand, Millie. Is there anything you can share with me . . . *anything at all?*"

"Just one hope, Lou."

"What?"

"I hope you have an Ace up your sleeve! The Ace of *Spades!*" (♠A)

Eighteen

'Demetri, I want to go over the situation with the upcoming *HerDeciMax* Advisory Committee meeting as well as the status of our Phase III trial once more before we adjourn this year's board of directors meeting." The person speaking was Anthony deCarlo, MD, a ten-year veteran of the Board and head of both the Corporate Governance and the Science and Technology Committees as well as a member of the Audit Committee.

Demetri Mihailov looked at his wristwatch, pursed his lips, and shook his head. Demetri was in his late fifties and a 20-year veteran of the pharmaceutical industry. He had begun his career as a medical practitioner in New Jersey, where he built a lucrative practice that he later sold to a major nationwide hospital system. His numerous contacts in and around Princeton drew him into the drug development business, and he rose quickly to such positions as Vice President for Research and Vice President for Clinical Studies until the position of President and Chief Executive Officer at BCaPharmaceutical beckoned. He now was in his third year at the company, and fighting to maintain the company's leadership position in the treatment of breast cancer.

It had been a difficult day. He was tired. His hair, dark gray with light highlights, was slightly unkempt, the result of running his fingers through it from time to time, more out of exasperation than anything else. Demetri already had shed the jacket of his tailored *Pelletier-Moreau* suit ($7,000), loosened his *Leveque* tie ($650), and had taken one shoe off (his pair of *Gravois* loafers cost $4000) to rub his toes after having been on his feet most of the day, giving presentations. Now, he stood up again, this time to respond to yet another question from Dr. Anthony deCarlo.

"Tony, Tony, Tony. We have been through these topics twice in the last two days. I thought we pretty well had wrung out our plan vis-à-vis Berranger. Hell, I've already put it into action." It was 8:30 PM. Demetri knew it would take at least another hour to go over the material deCarlo wanted to review, increasing the possibility that he would be late for his meeting with Tricia. *God help me if she gets pissed and says something to the authorities regarding Berranger or pushes me into a corner on this divorce matter!* Beads of sweat formed on his forehead.

"I know, Demetri, but we only have one more chance to stop *HerDeciMax* dead in its tracks. If it becomes the new standard of care, we're sunk. No two ways about it. Our drug goes off-patent in a year—"

"Tony! We've talked about this until we were blue in the face. Look, I've been doing everything I can to find a replacement for Broussard." Demetri took a paper napkin off the boardroom table and wiped his brow. He loosened his collar, sat down in his large swivel chair, put on his reading glasses, shuffled through the stacks of files in front of him, and pulled a large brown accordion folder from the bottom of one stack. "Okay, everyone, let's go through the *HerDeciMax* Advisory Committee situation one more time.

"If you will pull out my memorandum to the Board dated a day after Broussard's death in late March, you will see that I have convinced Dr. William Jeffries, who holds both an MD and a PhD in Biotechnology, to work with us. He currently is a Professor of Oncology at Escondido Southern University's Advanced Center for Biotechnology Research. Like Broussard, he has written in the past of his concerns relative to the safety profile of *HerDeciMax*, and has published several papers on the subject. He also has made a number of presentations at various symposia here and in Europe on the drug's safety profile. And—" Demetri paused for effect. "He's a good friend of the current FDA commissioner. In fact, they were just on the same panel at a symposium on breast cancer held in New Orleans a few weeks ago, and a friend told me that he saw them on the golf course together soon afterwards.

"Now, I'm not ignoring the fact that his views regarding *HerDeciMax* are in the minority. In fact, they have been discredited in some circles because they ignore the more robust statistical models that the FDA will be applying to the data Berranger is expected to release shortly. Regardless, all Jeffries has to do is sow enough uncertainty and doubt during the next *HerDeciMax* Advisory Committee meeting such that the FDA will refuse to approve Berranger's drug."

The board members spoke among themselves for a few minutes before deCarlo stood and addressed them. "I understand that, Demetri. But, as always, the hurdle we have to jump over is the one involving the approval of the waiver Jeffries must submit before he can be seated on the advisory committee. He's involved in one Phase II trial and one Phase III trial of drugs that, if approved, would compete with *HerDeciMax* in the breast cancer space. One of those drugs is *ours!* It's the one in Phase III. How does Jeffries get paid for his participation in these trials? Answer me that. There's only so much you can hide in a waiver request, you know!"

Demetri immediately jumped to his feet and pounded his fist on the boardroom table. "I've told you, Tony, time and time again. No money associated with either trial goes directly to Jeffries. We, and the pharmaceutical house that owns the drug in the Phase II trial—and I've spoken with their CEO—contracted with CROs to run the trials. In both cases, the CROs have issued grants to Dr. Jeffries' university. That's how Jeffries is 'taken care of'.

"I've already seen a draft of the waiver Jeffries will submit to the FDA for the *HerDeciMax* Advisory Committee meeting. It was prepared by our legal team as a way of, shall we say, extending a helping hand to the good doctor. Jeffries' waiver doesn't look any different, in general, from a hundred other waivers that have been submitted to, *and approved by,* the FDA in the last few years. Tony, I really think you're worrying about something that's a non-issue. Our people are on top of the situation. You have to trust me on this!"

Anthony deCarlo threw his hands into air. "This whole thing with the CROs makes me very nervous, Demetri...always has, always will. Look, I know it's difficult for the FDA to find people for these advisory committees who aren't in one way or another connected to major drug trials. But some researchers and medical practicioners are *so* involved in multiple studies involving new investigational drugs that the conflicts of interest fairly leap off the page, regardless of how they are masked. Members of the Senate Finance Committee have made this a subject of their investigations for several years now. They aren't going to give up! Sooner or later, the Committee will force the FDA to tighten up its policies and procedures for vetting advisory committee candidates."

"Tony, the FDA doesn't give a flying f#$% what the US Senate thinks! The agency has been thumbing its nose at Congress for years!"

"Yeah, well, God help us if something happens at one of these advisory committees that comes back to haunt us, Demetri! And I'm talking about a really big mess involving a conflict of interest so large that it catches the attention of the mainstream media and ends up with you and me being subpoenaed to testify before a Senate subcommittee!"

"Give me a break, Tony! Nothing like that is going to happen. While it's true some senators have called for higher levels of scrutiny, there's no indication they're going to be able to change things at the FDA anytime soon."

"Okay, okay. . . let's say you're right. But I'm still nervous. Think about this. I don't know about you, but it doesn't take a genius to connect the dots regarding what's happened over the last several days. First, that analyst over at Bartlett, Cline, and Stephenson. . . what the hell was his name?"

"Williamson."

"Yeah, Williamson. Thanks, Cheryl. Williamson gets murdered. He's the one who helped us keep a lid on Berranger's stock price over the last two years. That was critical, because it severely constrained Berranger's ability to raise money in the public markets. Remember how it slowed their ability to enroll patients in the Phase III trial of *HerDeciMax*. It gave us time to catch up . . . to get *BCa-1407* through Phase II and into Phase III.

"And then, Broussard was murdered in Washington . . . in exactly the same way. He was the one who created uncertainty regarding the safety and efficacy of *HerDeciMax* at the advisory committee meeting more than two years ago . . . uncertainty that resulted in the FDA asking for more data. That saved *our* hide and got the FDA off the hook. The last thing certain powerful people in the agency wanted, at the time, was to change the standard of care! Add to that the fact that Broussard was going to submit an application and a waiver in fulfillment of the requirements to participate in the upcoming *HerDeciMax* Advisory Committee meeting—which only was logical, given his participation on the previous advisory committee—and you can see how someone might have taken a distinct disliking to the man.

"Do you want my opinion, Demetri? I think someone is heaping vengeance upon the heads of people who played a part in delaying the approval of *HerDeciMax*. And the murders are going to continue until we back off and stop corrupting the FDA's drug approval process. Frankly, I'm beginning to worry that *my* head will be the next one to end up on a statue!"

"Have you lost your goddamn mind, Tony? We have no proof that the two murders are connected. They took place in two cities that are hundreds of miles apart, and the men who were murdered worked in two entirely different fields. Williamson covered 15, maybe 20, biotech companies. He made plenty of enemies, believe me. As for Broussard, he just might have been in the wrong place at the wrong time. Washington can be a dangerous city. And besides, what are you. . .*what are any of us*. . .going to do? The police in both cities are, I'm sure, working around the clock to solve the murders. We, on the other hand, have a company to save."

"Okay, Demetri. I'm not going to say another word about advisory committees." He sat down and thumbed through some folders in front of him. Then, deCarlo looked up. "But one more time, before we break up, please run us through the status of *BCa-1407*."

Demetri looked at his watch. He let out a sigh, and shook his head. "Okay. . .one more time. The trial is progressing on schedule. We had a hiccup last month when one of our suppliers received an FDA Form-483 following their most recent plant inspection. The supplier is seeking clarification of the issues raised by the FDA, but for now, they are unable to ship product to us. As a result, some of our trial centers faced the possibility of running low on *BCa-1407* within the next three weeks. We apprised the FDA of this problem and offered to work with both the supplier and the FDA to resolve the matter as quickly as possible.

"When I was notified that our supplier had received a Form-483, I immediately instructed our vice presidents for Biopharmaceutical Businesses and for Manufacturing to accelerate the qualification of already-identified secondary sources for the reagents[32] we needed. I did this not only to address our current requirements, but also, to ensure that we would not experience these problems in the future.

---

32 A reagent is a substance or compound that is added to a system in order to bring about a chemical reaction.

"I have been told, as I noted in my presentation yesterday, that we *will* have a qualified secondary source in place Monday. The new supplier currently has a certified facility meeting FDA Good Manufacturing Practices. Our people in Manufacturing tell me that while it will be close, they are absolutely certain that they can catch up with the demands of the Phase III trial by the end of next week. So, that being the case, let me be absolutely clear. We *will* meet all of our commitments to the trial centers. There will be *no* interruptions in the trial.

"This never should have happened, of course. I take full responsibility for not having a secondary source for the reagents, on line and providing product in parallel with our primary supplier. I'm afraid this is one instance where my cost-cutting efforts went a little too far. Recall, however, that last year, my efforts had a *significant* impact on our bottom line, which, let me remind you, did *not* go unnoticed by Wall Street. I didn't see any of you ladies and gentlemen complaining then! As I recall, our stock jumped more than $2 after quarterly results were announced last November!"

"So, you're saying, Demetri, that everything is proceeding on schedule with the Phase III trial of *BCa-1407*?" Anthony deCarlo simply would not let Mihailov off the hook. "The fate of this company rests on the success of *BCa-1407*. If we don't receive approval for it before *PCaP* goes off-patent, we might as well wallpaper the men's 'john' with our stock certificates!"

"Dammit, Tony, I can't give you any guarantees. There are no guarantees in life. We're dealing with human beings, here. Each patient in the trial...at least each patient who is receiving *BCa-1407*...is going to respond to the drug in a slightly different way. The pharmakinetics[33] will be different in each case, as you know, as will the side effects. Who knows, when the data are finally analyzed, whether or not the drug will meet the agreed-to end-points for the trial? I don't have a crystal ball. All we can do is hope—and pray—that *BCa-1407* confirms the data that we saw in the Phase II trial, which were very encouraging!"

The room was silent, except for the noise a few participants made while they stuffed briefing papers and charts into their briefcases.

Finally, deCarlo spoke. "Thanks, Demetri. I appreciate your taking the time this evening. I don't have anything more for the Board."

"Thanks, Tony.

"Well, if there's no more business to conduct, I want to thank everyone for a very productive board meeting. I wish you all a good evening, and safe travels, wherever the road may take you."

33 Pharmakinetics is the process by which a drug is absorbed, distributed, metabolized, and eliminated by the body.

Nineteen

It was 9:25 PM when Demetri was finally able to say his 'good byes' to the board members, run to his office, throw a few things into his briefcase that he would need over his extended weekend with Tricia, and take the elevator to the building's basement garage. The underground parking levels were deserted at this hour, and it took only a moment for him to sprint to his car from the elevator door. He had just taken delivery of the gray Mercedes-Benz SLR McLaren Gullwing while he waited on the delivery of his SLS-AMG, which was due to be delivered in mid-2011. The SLR McLaren he had ordered set him back $450,000, but he didn't care...that was less than 5% of his annual salary, and that did *not* include his bonus, which was substantial. *I wonder how the 'little people' are getting by these days,* he chortled to himself as he lifted the driver's-side door, threw his briefcase in the back, and settled into the rich black leather driver's seat. The car could do 0-60 mph in less than 3.6 seconds and had a top speed of 220 miles per hour. *Maybe, just maybe, we'll find some good roads out on Long Island this weekend where I can let this baby 'run',* he thought, as he pushed the START button.

The hand-built, 5.4L, 24-valve, supercharged, all-aluminum, SOHC V8 engine roared to life. As he slowly backed from his reserved parking space, he had only one thing on his mind: mollifying Tricia the next three days while he optimized his strategies for stopping Berranger's *HerDeciMax* and, at the same time, pushing the approval of his company's drug, *BCa-1407,* through the FDA. Once those two issues were resolved, he'd *think* about talking with his wife regarding a divorce...if Tricia didn't upset the applecart first!

Demetri drove up the exit lanes of the parking garage as quickly as he could, pitting himself and the Gullwing against the steep upward-spiraling ramp as it climbed three levels to the East Side of Central Park South. Tires screeching, he 'burned rubber' all the way to the street. His nostrils flared as he reveled in the sheer power in his grip. Racing around Columbus Circle, he headed uptown on Broadway, weaving in and out of traffic as he sped towards 79th Street. Once there, he turned right and worked his way to the 79th Street Transverse, then took the access road that led to the delivery dock behind the Delacourt Theater in Central Park.

Demetri was far too preoccupied to notice the car that had followed him ever since he left his office building. It would have been much easier to spot, had the driver not replaced the burned-out left, front headlight earlier that day. But now, with traffic on Broadway heavy even at this hour, and with taxicabs darting in and out of traffic, he hardly took notice that he was being followed.

He pulled into the theater's loading dock area at 9:45 PM—fifteen minutes prior to the time he was to meet Tricia—turned off the ignition, popped the driver's side door, and stepped out. A stiff wind was blowing through the park, forcing him to reach inside the car for his overcoat, which he immediately threw around his shoulders. It took only a few seconds for him to light a cigarette, and then, he stood looking up at the Manhattan skyline.

His concentration was broken when another car drove into the loading area, pulling to the right of the Gullwing and even with its front bumper. The driver jumped out and greeted Demetri with a smile. "Hi! Man, am I glad to see you! The guy I was talking to a few minutes ago told me to come up Third Avenue, turn left on 79th Street, cross through Central Park, and take the first right to the Henry Hudson Parkway...he said it would get me to the George Washington Bridge. He also said that from there, I could pick up the Interstate heading south towards New Jersey, and eventually, I would run into the Pennsylvania Turnpike. Well, doggone it, I musta missed a turn somewhere. How you guys in the Big Apple find your way around is beyond me!"

Cupping his hands, the young driver lit a filterless cigarette with match, inhaled deeply, threw his head back, and blew the smoke into the air. "God, is it always this windy?" He picked a piece of tobacco off his tongue.

Demetri just looked at him. "Well, the wind shows no mercy at this time of year, my friend. And they could have given you better directions. You're in the *middle* of Central Park. The 'right turn' you should make is further down 79th Street, much closer to the river.

"Where are you from, anyway?"

"Iowa, sir. Around Audubon, about an hour's drive west of Des Moines. Ever heard of the place?"

"No, can't say that I have. So, what brings you to New York?"

"Well, sir, I drove my little sister here so she could try out for some parts on Broadway. She loved taking acting courses in high school, and she dances a little, too. But what with us having no money and her not being able to go to college, she thought maybe she could waitress during the day and try out for some plays when the opportunities arose . . . even if it was for bit parts and such."

Demetri drummed the fingers of his left hand on his pants and looked at his watch. *Damn it, where is Trish? Maybe if she got here, I could get rid of this hayseed.* He took a long drag on his cigarette, which he was holding in his right hand, held the smoke for a few seconds, and exhaled. "Your sister must be very ambitious. I like that in a person. I wish her luck.

"Well, listen, don't feel bad about missing the turn. This isn't the easiest city to navigate. I'm sure almost everyone who doesn't live here has missed the exit to the Hudson River Parkway, first time around."

"Well, still and all, sir, I do need to get back to Iowa. I work hourly at the meat packing plant in Audubon, and if I'm not working, I don't get paid. We don't even get personal leave . . . nothing. I'm lucky if I clear $20,000 a year after taxes, Social Security, and Medicare, and that's with some overtime on Saturdays, if the demand is there. I have a piece of paper here, and a pencil. If you could draw a little map, I'll be out of your hair real quick." The young man started to walk toward Demetri.

"Sure . . . give me the paper and pencil. Happy to help." *For God's sake! And this guy's in a hurry to get back to his job at a meat packing plant in Iowa? Give me a break. I'd kill myself if that's all I had to look forward to every day!*

It was the last thought Demetri Mihailov ever had.

<u>Twenty</u>

*T*ricia Fournier was running late. It was one of *those* days, though it did begin on a positive note. Tim Miles met with her at 7 AM, apprising her of the fact that both their e-mail and backup e-mail servers had been cleansed of all e-mails she wanted deleted. "The e-mails haven't just been deleted, Ms. Fournier. . .I've overwritten all of the memory locations where the e-mails had been stored three times. It took me all day and night after we talked, but working alone with some software I've been testing, I was able to complete the job an hour earlier than expected. There is no one. . .*NO ONE*. . .who could ever find even a trace of one e-mail that previously had been the subject of interest in this matter!

"And we're just about done cleansing all of your staff's computers and memory devices, here and at their apartments, of the material you wanted erased. My team is working on the last computers now, and we'll be finished by noon."

"Thanks, Tim. You can be sure I'll take care of you and your team at the end of the year! Great work."

Unfortunately, Tricia Fournier's day went downhill soon after the meeting with Tim. One of the biotech companies that her analysts followed, Molecular Transcription Technologies, which had a drug, *MTT-569,* in Phase III testing, announced before the start of trading that the FDA's Drug Safety Oversight Board, by a vote of 13 to 2, called for the company to immediately suspend the clinical trial of its drug at *all* sites throughout the United States. Data that had been made available to the Board showed an imbalance of deaths between the two treatment arms, with a higher death rate in the treatment arm receiving *MTT-569* than in the arm receiving the placebo. In pre-market trading, Molecular Transcription Technologies' stock was down $15, from $27 to $12, and it was still dropping when Tricia called an emergency meeting of her staff at 8:15 AM.

"Dammit, Steve, what the hell was Williamson thinking when he put out a 'Buy' on Molecular Transcription Technologies? You worked for him. What was in his mind? I distinctly remember telling him that we couldn't expect more than mediocre results from the Phase III trial. And the consensus on the Street was that, at best, the results of the trial would be good, but not overwhelmingly so. He never should have put out anything more than a rating of 'Neutral, Market Perform'.

"I just got a call from one of our largest institutional clients, and they are *not* happy. We may lose them as a client. And this will *not* be the only call like that I'm going to get today, you can bet on it!

"I want you, Steve, to lead a team of analysts that includes Maura, Ellen, and Barry. Go over *every single recommendation* we have outstanding for the stocks we cover. Compare them with the consensus on the Street for each company, and align our positions with the crowd. Until I can bring in some heavy-duty talent to manage the analyst side of the house, we're going to play it very conservatively. I know biotechs are risky and S#$% happens, but if we suffer one more of these surprises—and in Phase III, for God's sake—we'll lose most of our institutional clients, assuming we still have any COB today. Now get to work. I want your recommendations on my desk before I leave work!"

Jacobs nodded. Everyone saw he was still depressed over seeing his colleague's severed head stuck on the horn of the Wall Street Bull a week earlier. They knew it would be difficult for him to concentrate. They also knew, and accepted the fact, that the bulk of the work would fall to them, so they moved off as a team to complete the assignment.

Fournier spent the remainder of the day responding to angry telephone calls and e-mails from her institutional clients. The angriest were from those that had been 'long' Molecular Transcription Technologies stock—that is, owned the shares. In some cases, these institutions held a million shares or more, representing investments valued in the tens of millions of dollars. By the end of the normal trading day—4 PM, Eastern Standard Time—after dipping to a low of $9.78, the stock of Molecular Transcription Technologies had recovered some, closing at $13.48. However, in after-hours trading, it again was hit with a wave of selling. By 8 PM, when the after-market closed, the stock was again below $10, closing at $9.89.

Fournier was exhausted. She had not eaten a good lunch, snacking only on cold sandwiches, potato chips, and cookies that her executive assistant purchased for her in the company cafeteria. She had almost forgotten about meeting Demetri until she glanced up at her wall clock and saw that it was 9:40 PM. *Damn. Now I'm going to have to tell him I can't get away . . . I need to be here tomorrow to put out these fires!* Grabbing her overcoat, she took one sip of cold coffee, threw the cup across the room, and rushed out the door.

At the elevator, she repetitiously pushed the call button, watching as one elevator slowly climbed to the eleventh floor. The door had barely opened when she rushed onboard. Punching the 'L4' parking button, she tapped her foot as the elevator made its slow, measured way to the parking deck. She squeezed through the opening as the doors parted and ran to her car, hitting the door button on her remote from 20 feet away. Once inside, she put the key in the ignition, turned it, put the car in 'D', and sped up four levels to the street, where she headed uptown to meet Demetri.

Come on, come on, get the hell out of my way. There were cabs everywhere, a sea of yellow, weaving in and out like fish swimming upstream during spawning season...each one jockeying for a better position...stopping here and there to discharge or pick up a passenger...cutting her off to make a lane change, if only to save one or two seconds. The traffic light changed, and before she could move her car, the driver of the taxi in back of her hit his horn, making her even more frenzied. *One more time with the horn, you sonofabitch, and I'll put it where the Sun doesn't shine!*

No matter what lane she chose, it turned out to be the slowest. By 10 PM, she still was five minutes from the Delacourt Theater. *Demetri will have a fit...he's neurotic about punctuality.* She pressed on, pushing the speedometer as high as she dared, but not so high as to attract the attention of New York's Finest.

Finally, she turned right on West 79th Street and left onto the access road leading to the Delacourt Theater. A few seconds later, she pulled up behind the Mercedes. *Ah, there he is...in that new toy he just purchased. God, these men and their toys!* She pulled up behind him, turned off her ignition, stepped out, and walked up to the driver's side of the Mercedes.

"Demetri! Demetri! Hey, it's me, Trish." *Hmmm . . . he's sleeping.* She knocked on the window with the knuckle of the forefinger of her right hand. No response. "Come on, Demetri, quit screwing around. I know I'm a few minutes late."

No response.

All right, have it your way.

She reached down, grabbed the Gullwing's door handle, and opened the door. In an instant, Demetri's head rolled down the side of the seat, out the door, and onto her shoes, bathing her *Russo Giordano* alligator boots ($16,000) in blood. Demetri's eyes stared blankly up at her, his tongue lolling out the right side of his mouth.

The police said that Ms. Fournier was screaming insanely when the first NYPD cruiser arrived on the scene, three minutes after a man   they did not know who—placed a call to '911'. She was still screaming ten minutes later, when the paramedics arrived. It took them another ten minutes to sedate and stabilize her so that she could be transported to a hospital.

Twenty-one

'**W**ell, well, if it isn't my old friend, Louis Martelli, master detective of the New York Police Department. What kept you so long, Sarge? I would have thought that by now, if you heard a head drop anywhere within the city limits of Manhattan, you would have swooped in by helicopter within two minutes of the murder!"

Michael Antonetti, Deputy Coroner, simply could *not* resist sticking it to his old friend. Michael was on his knees next to the black Mercedes Gullwing near the loading dock of the Delacourt Theater, looking at a head with eyes staring up at him. The CSI with him, Robin Peterson, a flirt who wore her flaming red hair long, stringy, and parted in the middle, already had documented the site.

"Hi, ya, Martelli. I hear you and Michael often meet like this. Everybody at Headquarters is talking about you two, ya know!" She could barely stifle her laugh.

Martelli rose to the occasion. "Heads are popping up all over the place, Red. If it weren't for them, none of us would have anything to do with our time. Be thankful you have a job in this stinkin' economy! And frankly, if I didn't know any better, I'd think you were the one knocking off these guys, just so you'd have something to do at night. From what I've heard, you don't seem to have many dates these days!"

Robin threw her pen at him, but missed because she was laughing so hard. "That's bad karma, *Defective* Martelli!" Robin loved to play with words. She had once called Lou an 'incontinent defective' during their morning intake briefing after Lou failed to return something to the Evidence Room. The comment cracked everyone up so much, including their boss, that it saved Lou from a severe tongue lashing.

"Hey, Red, I resemble that remark!"

Antonetti was beside himself with laugher. "Well, at least it's not 4 AM in the damn morning, like the last time, Lou. The perp did us a favor this time. Maybe we'll get home and to bed before 2 AM! Hey, Red, hold this evidence bag for me so that I can stuff the head into it."

Martelli watched as Antonetti carefully placed the head in the evidence bag, sealed it, and wrote something on the frosted label with his pen. "So, Red, what do we know about the vic?"

"The guy's name is Demetri Mihailov and—"

"I'm not surprised," interrupted Martelli. "Actually, I've almost been wondering when this was going to happen."

Antonetti and Peterson cocked their heads and looked up, quizzically.

"My investigation showed he might be a prime target.

"I truly believe whoever committed the three murders has now accomplished what he set out to do. I think he considered the three men he murdered the 'horsemen' of an apocalypse[34] that was visited upon someone for whom he cared deeply. This was his way of exacting revenge. And having done that, I think

---

34 http://www.gotquestions.org/four-horsemen-apocalypse.html

he's left the area and headed home, most likely last night, and most likely to Iowa."

Antonetti looked Lou in the eye. "And you deduced this *how?*"

"Well, long story short, all three men were connected to efforts intended to stop the approval of a new drug for the treatment of a certain type of breast cancer. I think I have the evidence I need, now, to connect most of the dots. What I don't have is something definitive that will lead me to the *specific* person who committed the crimes.

"I'm hoping that someone saw what happened here tonight. I know there are homeless in the area. And there's a security camera mounted on top of the theater, though God knows if it's working. During the off-season, the surveillance systems in areas like this don't always get the maintenance they need. We'll see. But still, I have to believe that someone saw something.

"Was there anyone around when the first patrol car showed up?"

Peterson pointed to an NYPD cruiser parked near the loading dock. "That was the first car on the scene. I think the officer's name is Murtaugh."

"Thanks, I'll talk with him." Lou turned and walked back to where the officer was standing.

"Officer Murtaugh, do you have a minute? I'm Detective Lou Martelli, NYPD."

"Sure, Detective, how can I help you?"

"I understand you were the first patrolman on the scene. What can you tell me?"

"Well, I received a call around 10:10 PM from Dispatch regarding a murder in the parking lot and a woman screaming.

Dispatch said that the caller was a male but that he provided no additional information beyond alerting to the murder. I arrived three minutes later, but there was no one here except the woman...and a head on the ground next to the driver's side of the Mercedes. The woman was in pretty bad shape. I immediately called Dispatch for a 'bus'. Turns out Dispatch already had called for one, and it arrived a minute later. It took the paramedics quite a while to stop the woman from screaming. Man, I've never heard anything like it. Then the coroner showed up, so the other officers and I let him and the CSI take over. I'm just completing the paperwork now."

"Thanks, Officer. Would you mind making sure I get a copy of your report when you file it? Here's my card."

"Not a problem, Detective."

"Thanks."

Martelli turned and limped back to where Antonetti and Peterson were still working. "So, Peterson, can you fill me in? How do you see this going down?"

"Well, we don't know how the suspect actually committed the crime, except to say, of course, that he severed the head from the body quite cleanly...most likely using a professional butcher knife."

"Lou," interrupted Antonetti, "the cut is clean, just like the one we saw on Williamson's neck."

"And," continued Peterson, "the murder took place here." She pointed to the ground next to the driver's side of the Mercedes. "You can see where the body bled out while the suspect,"—she started to back up, motioning Martelli to follow her—"carried the head around the back of car, opened the passenger-side door, and reached across the passenger seat to lodge it between the headrest behind the driver's seat and the window. I found a blood trail to support that theory.

"Then, it looks like he dragged the body by its feet over here—to where he had apparently parked *his* vehicle to the right of the Mercedes—and dumped the body into the trunk. At that point, he left the scene. You can see the bloody tire tracks. I have photographs and contact copies of the tread marks, so we can match them to the car's tires, if we ever locate the vehicle. I'll run the tires for make and model.

"One only can guess what he did with the body. But given how cleanly he severed the head, I'd say he stopped somewhere, chopped the guy up, and threw the pieces into the Hudson River. That would be the easiest thing for him to do. I doubt he would take the time to bury the pieces. Too much risk that someone would see him."

Martelli nodded. "Yeah . . . makes sense. The guy appears to be a real whiz with knives. Thanks, Peterson."

Lou stroked his chin. *I wonder if the guy who made the '911' call witnessed the murder. Given the homeless population around here, someone had to see what happened. But who? And how do I get them to talk with me?*

"Michael, I'm heading home. I have an idea, but first I need to get a good night's sleep. I've been going 18 and 19 hours a day since the first murder, and it's catching up with me. Thanks for your help! I'll be looking for your report."

"You'll have it, Lou. Good luck tomorrow."

"Take care. See ya, Peterson."

Twenty-two

'Hey, sailor! Would you like to have a good time?" It was Stephanie. She had just rolled over to Lou's side of their bed and had propped his left eye open with the thumb of her left hand. Lou stared blankly into the darkness. "Helloooooo," Stephanie cooed, kissing him on the lips. "Anyone home? The kids are still asleep, sailor."

Suddenly Lou reached up and grabbed her, gave her a big kiss, and mockingly corrected her. "How many times have I told you, Baby? It's *Master Sergeant Martelli*?" He tickled her until she could barely breathe.

"Lou! Stop it! Stop it! We're going to wake the children!" She was laughing hysterically.

"You're the one who's making all the noise, Baby!

"Look, I love you, Sweetheart, but I need to get up and out to the Delacourt Theater in Central Park. I want to be there before the sun comes up. Believe me, there's nothing more I want to do right now than make love to you. But we had a homicide out there last night . . . another beheading. The MO fits the one we had a few days ago on Wall Street as well as the one in DC."

"These cases are the toughest I think you've ever had, Lou. But if you can't solve them, no one can."

"Thanks for the vote of confidence! But I'm missing one piece of important information. I had an idea last night, and I want to try something this morning. Maybe it'll work, maybe it won't. If it does, it'll break these cases wide open."

He got out of bed, grabbed his boxer shorts, and hopped into the bathroom to shower and shave. Stephanie turned over and went back to sleep. The time was 5 AM.

Twenty minutes later, she sensed someone was staring at her. She turned over, opened her eyes, and saw Master Sergeant Louis Martelli standing at the foot of her bed in his Army fatigues. The insignia he wore was that of the Army's Third Aviation Regiment of the Third Infantry Division based at Fort Stewart, Georgia.

"Why are you dressed that way, Lou? I haven't seen you in uniform since you left Walter Reed Army Medical Center on your last day in the Army."

"The edge of the service area where we found the body is overgrown with trees and brush. I need to scout around a bit to see if I can find some evidence. And I certainly don't want to ruin a good business suit in the process. Besides, a number of the homeless live in that area. Many used to be in the military. Some still dress in old fatigues, though I'm sure they got them at the Goodwill or some other agency serving the homeless. I didn't see any homeless at the back of the theater last night. They have an aversion to the police, as you can imagine, and God knows, enough police were out there last night to take care of a small city. So, I figure, if I go looking dressed more or less like one of them, someone who may have seen something might be willing to talk with me."

"Well, it can't hurt, Darling. It might be a good idea to take my car."

"Good thought, Steph. Wouldn't make sense to drive up in that big Ford with antennas sticking out the back deck. See if you can get a ride to work this morning. And tell the kids they'll just have to suck it up and 'take one' for the NYPD. . .it's the bus for them, this morning. And I don't want to hear any whining from them when I get home tonight. It's not the end of the world! If I hear whining at the dinner table, *that* will be the end of the world! *Theirs!* And you can tell them that."

"Gotcha, Sarge! I'll take care of it. *You* keep your mind on the road. You've only been getting five to six hours of sleep a night for the past week—don't think I haven't noticed. That does *not* make you the kind of person with whom I want to be on the road."

"I hear you, Baby."

Twenty-three

*L*ou climbed into his wife's 2005 Buick, backed out their driveway, and headed into Manhattan through the Brooklyn Battery Tunnel. Once in the City, he headed uptown to Central Park...to the site of the previous night's crime scene. The trip to the loading dock at the rear of the Delacourt Theater took almost 30 minutes, despite the early hour, due in part to an accident at the entrance to the tunnel. Martelli pulled behind the building just as the first light of the day illuminated the low clouds on the eastern horizon. The air was still. The only sound he heard was a lone mocking bird.

He got out of the car and began examining the grounds. Walking along the edge of the service area, he stopped now and then to poke at the dirt around the base of bushes and shrubs, checking the ground for anything that might have blown off the pavement. A search of the large trash containers on the site yielded nothing.

Fifteen minutes passed. Lou was about to give up when he decided to do one more search of the area where the Mercedes had been parked. As he started to lower himself to the ground on one knee, he heard footsteps behind him.

"Hey, Sarge, can you spare a buck for a vet?"

Lou turned around to see a homeless person he estimated to be in his early sixties. It was difficult to say. The man had a salt-and-pepper scrub beard, bloodshot eyes, looked as if he had not bathed in weeks, and wore recent-issue Army fatigues that obviously had been given to him by one of the many shelters that dotted the City. The insignia on the uniform were those of a corporal, and the unit patch was that of the First Calvary Division, Fort Hood, Texas.

"Sure, Corporal." Lou reached for his wallet and took out a $20 bill.

"Actually, it's sergeant, Sarge...Sergeant Luke Sanders." The man looked at the ground and a tear rolled down his cheek. "Sergeant Luke Sanders, Charlie Company of 1st Battalion, 20th Infantry Regiment, 11th Brigade, 23rd Infantry Division."

Whew, thought Martelli. *That's the outfit that was involved in the My Lai Massacre in March 1968...the mass murder of 500 unarmed citizens in South Vietnam, all civilians and a majority of women, children—including babies—and elderly people.* "I've heard of Charlie Company, Sarge. That was a pretty rough situation in My Lai."[35]

Sanders broke down, sobbing. "I ain't never talked to anyone about it to this day, Sarge. We came into this village, and God, it was impossible to tell who was a friend and who was the enemy. Everyone was suspect. The men just went crazy. I tried to reason with the officers...Calley, among them. But they just kept shooting. It didn't matter whether they was women or children." Sanders was sobbing uncontrollably, his entire body heaving.

Lou reached out and put both arms around the man's shoulders to comfort him. "I saw one man shoot at a baby with

---

35 http://en.wikipedia.org/wiki/My_Lai_Massacre

a .45. He missed, so he moved closer and tried again. He missed that time, too, so he walked up to the baby and shot again. This time he hit him right in the head. I got so sick, I went into the brush and puked my guts out. When the shooting stopped, none of the villagers was alive."

It took five minutes for the man to calm down. Finally, he pulled back, took out a dirty handkerchief, and wiped his eyes. "I'm sorry, Sarge. I guess it took 42 years and the sight of your uniform to finally. . .*finally*. . .release me from my personal Hell. The docs down at Walter Reed tried to help me, but what I saw in Viet Nam was so terrible. . .well, there was nothin' they could do for me. I could barely talk about what happened. They gave me medication to help me sleep, but it was five years before the nightmares stopped. I went from job to job, never able to hold one for more than a few months. I met a nice lady, but even that didn't last. It's like I died that day in My Lai along with all those people. Most, probably, were innocent."

Lou took out his wallet, and pulled $328 from it. "Here, Sarge. Check yourself into a hotel, clean yourself up, have a good meal, buy yourself some nice clothes. Then, tomorrow morning, get down to the VA and tell them you need their help. Let them work with you to put your life back together."

"Thanks, Sarge. You don't know how much this means to me." He stopped and hung his head, barely able to speak. "So many people have passed me by when I needed help.

"But what happened to you? I saw that you walk with a limp."

"Aw, it's nothin', Sarge. My wife whacked me with a broomstick last night for chasing after other women." They laughed, probably the first time that Sanders had laughed in 42 years.

"Actually, Luke, I'm with the New York Police Department. My name is Lou Martelli. I'm a detective with the Homicide Division.

"You may have noticed some activity around here last night. We had a murder. Now, we're not sure where it actually occurred. But we found the head of a man on the ground next to his car back near the loading area. You didn't see anything, did you?"

"Hell, yes, Sarge! A woman, who, I think, came to meet the victim, screamed so loud, you could have heard her at the other end of the Park! I was watchin' her from the bushes behind the theater when she drove up. She parked behind the Mercedes Gullwing—don't see many like that one—got out, and walked to the driver's door. After tapping on the window and getting no response, she reached down and pulled up the door. The guy's head dropped on her shoes. There was blood everywhere. That's when I scrambled over to the payphone to the front of the theater, hit '911', and called the police. Then I disappeared, if you know what I mean. I could hear the woman screaming all the way through the trees behind the theater and beyond."

"As I understand it, Luke, she was still screaming when the police arrived three minutes after your call. She's in the hospital now, under heavy sedation. The docs tell us it will be days before we can talk with her—if ever."

"What does that mean, Lou?"

"I'm not sure, but the docs say that sometimes, in cases like this, people *never* recover. . . that they spend the rest of their days in an institution."

"That poor woman!"

"Given what you saw, Luke, I certainly can understand your wanting to get out of there. But forgive me, I have to ask. Did you see anything *before* the woman opened the car door?"

"You bet! The guy pulled up in his Mercedes around 9:45 PM, drove to the far back of the lot, stopped, and got out. He lit up a cigarette, and was putting his lighter away when another car drove up, and parked to the right of the Mercedes."

"Did you happen to recognize the make, model, and year of the second car, Luke?"

"It's hard to tell these days, Lou. . .not like the old days, when I was growing up. Then, each manufacturer's product had its own distinctive 'look'. You could tell a Packard from a Ford and a Pontiac from a Studebaker in a heartbeat. Those were the days, huh, Lou? But I'd say it definitely was an American car, maybe a Chevy. . .something around late 1980s, or so. The car looked pretty beat up. And I noticed that when the guy pulled in, the front license plate was covered, maybe with a piece of cardboard."

"Okay, that's great, Luke. Please, go on— No, wait a minute. . .did you happen to notice whether or not the left, front headlight was burned out?"

"Nope. . .both headlights were 'on' when he pulled in, that's for sure. I would have remembered if one of them was burned out."

Just great! thought Martelli. *We can thank the DCPD for that. Now it'll be even more difficult to find this guy on the roads!* "Okay. Thanks. Go ahead. I'm sorry I interrupted you."

"That's okay. Anyway, this guy stepped out—"

"What did he look like, Luke?"

"I'd say he was about six feet tall...had light-colored hair. From the way he moved, I'd say he was on the young side...maybe in his twenties. But I couldn't see his face clearly.

"Anyway, he lights up, too, and they start talking. They chatted for, maybe, three or four minutes, nice and casual, like. All of a sudden, the young guy takes out a big syringe...I mean, this thing was huge. You could use it on a cow or horse, or something. He jams the syringe into the other guy's chest. Well, before the guy can even cry out, he collapses in a heap like a sack of potatoes.

"The guy now takes out this huge knife and slashes the guy on the ground across the throat. Before you know it, the guy's head is on the ground and the killer is draggin' the body to his car. He opened the trunk and stuffed the body into it. Then, he ran back, took the head, ran around the Mercedes, and reaching in from the passenger side, propped the head between the headrest and the window on the driver's side so it would appear, from the outside, that the guy was dozing in the driver's seat.

"I could see all of this very clearly because when he lifted the car's passenger-side door, the inside lights came on. I even got a glimpse of the murderer's face...he definitely was young, and he had dirty blonde hair."

Lou pulled the sketch drawn by the DC police artist from the pocket of his jacket, unfolded it, and showed it to the sergeant. "Is this the man, Luke?"

"Yes! The eyes should be a little closer together, Lou, but I'd recognize him anywhere. He's the one!"

"That's good, Luke. There's no doubt, now, that he's the man I've been chasing since this all began over a week ago. But you were saying?"

"Then, the murderer ran to his car and took off, burnin' rubber like you wouldn't believe. I'd say the whole thing, from the time he cut the guy's head off until he left the parking lot, took less than two minutes. The guy with the knife knew exactly what he was doing, Sarge."

"Believe me, Luke, the guy knows knives! We think he worked in either a butcher shop or a meat market...maybe even on a farm.

"But why didn't you call '911' right after you saw the guy commit the murder and leave?"

"I was going to do that Lou, but I was stunned. It took me a minute to realize what I had seen. Then the woman drove up just as I was going to head for the payphone on the side of the theater. So, I held back."

"I understand, Luke. Tell me, you seem to have a keen eye for detail...did you get a number off the license plate on the murderer's car?"

"Well, Sarge, it was pretty dark, and I was keeping back, keeping outta sight—"

"I hear you, brother!"

"I mean, the last thing I needed was for the guy to come after me!"

"Of course."

"Anyway, I stayed in the shadows...stood very still. And just as the guy pulled out, the light from the security lamp on the loading dock reflected off his rear plate, and I was able to grab the numbers and letters. I guess the cardboard musta blown off in the wind. Here, I scribbled the number on this piece of paper." He pulled a dirty scrap of paper from his pants pocket. On it were written three numbers and three letters. He handed the piece of paper to Martelli.

Lou stared at what he saw. It took him a few seconds to make out the numbers and letters. Sanders' handwriting was that of a child's, given that he probably had not written much of anything for years.

Well I'll be go to Hell! thought Lou. "Luke, this is the break I have been waiting for! I need to get back to my office immediately. I think you just broke the case for me. I can't thank you enough. Jump in! I'm going to take you to a good hotel, and then, I'm heading for my office. But I'll need you to come down to the station tomorrow to give a statement to one of our detectives. Do you think you can do that? Ask for Detective Sean O'Keeffe. He'll send a car for you. Here, I'll write it on my card. I'll make sure he knows to expect you. Okay, Luke?"

"You bet! I'll be there!

"And Lou . . . thank you. You saved my life."

"Thank *you*, Sarge. You cracked my case!"

Twenty-four

*A*fter dropping Sergeant Luke Sanders at a hotel on Manhattan's West Side, Martelli headed downtown to his office at police headquarters. Picking up his cellphone, he selected Missy Dugan's office icon and hit SEND. He heard Missy's voice and was about to interrupt when it became apparent he was listening to her 'greeting'. "Hi. This is Missy Dugan, Principal Information Technology Specialist with the New York Police Department. I can't take your call right now, but if you'll leave your name and number, I'll call you as soon as possible. Thanks! And have a great day. *Beep*."

"Missy, this is Martelli! I pay you a big six-figure salary to be at the phone 24x7. I'm docking your pay $10,000 for screwing around with your electronic toys while the rest of us are out here, bustin' our humps chasin' the bad guys. Call me! Out!"

He had no sooner terminated the call when the device began 'ringing' with the song he had assigned to incoming calls from Missy. . . *My Life Would Suck Without You.*[36]

"Lou, dammit, something's going to get busted, all right, and it won't be your hump! More like your 'johnson'! And the

---

36 *My Life Would Suck Without You* is a song performed by American pop rock singer-songwriter Kelly Clarkson.

last time I checked my automated deposit, you must have fat-fingered my net pay because the balance looked like S#$%!"

"Ah, is that the sweet voice of my turtle dove? Look, sweetheart, I have the license plate number for our perp . . . the guy who's been leaving heads around New York and Washington. I'm on my way to the office. Please pull that CD we should have gotten from the Iowa Motor Vehicle Division by now . . . we did get it, right? I think it should tell us who we're looking for."

"Yeah, we got the FedEx package. The guy in the mailroom rushed it down to the lab the minute he finished signing for it. Give me the license plate information. I'll run the plate for you right now. I have the CD queued up on my computer's drive."

"Okay . . . here it is." Lou read her the three numbers, followed by the three letters.

"Got it. Stand by.

"Bingo! I have your guy, Lou. The car is registered in Audubon County, Iowa." She proceeded to give Lou the name on the registration.

He took a deep breadth. "Thanks, Missy. That's the 'Ace of *Spades*'! (♠A) I just drew a Royal Flush!"

"What?"

"I'll explain later, doll face! I need to make a call as soon as I get to my office. I'm pulling into the parking garage now. This is a case I'll *never* forget."

"Okay, Lou. Congratulations! It's always great to work with you."

"I couldn't have done this without you, Mis. You're the best!"

Twenty-five

'Guthrie County Constable's Office, Officer Lake, speaking. Please hold...I'm sorry. I had another incoming call. This is Officer Lake. How may I direct your call?"

"Good morning, Officer Lake, this is Homicide Detective Lou Martelli of the New York Police Department. Is Constable Hutchinson in?" Lou was absolutely ebullient.

"Oh, good morning, sir. Yes, I'll put you right through to him."

"Good morning, Lou. How are you this fine day? The snow is *finally* starting to melt out here, which for us is just the greatest sight! Maybe we'll be able to plant by August." He laughed. "Now the only thing we have to worry about is the flooding."

"It's always something, isn't it, Brad? But it *is* a fine day...at least for the NYPD. I believe—and *believe* is the operative word—that we've finally identified our killer. He hails from your neck of the woods. But I don't think he presents a danger to anyone out there."

"Sounds like you did a great job, Lou. I'm impressed with you and the NYPD. What can you tell me?"

Lou gave the constable a brief overview of his findings and the identity of the suspect.

"Damn!"

"What's that, Brad?"

"Now I recognize the man in the sketch, Lou. I should have realized who it was before now. But the eyes didn't register. Doggone it! I just couldn't place the face! Besides, I haven't seen the boy for quite a few years.

"I'm not surprised by what you tell me, Lou. I heard from Millie over in Des Moines that he was furious, absolutely beside himself, when he read what had happened in Washington at the advisory committee meeting.

"He's the foster kid, by the way, who lived on the Holtzmann farm for several years and who read whenever he had a spare moment. I recall, now that you said his name, how everyone was so proud of him for his accomplishments in the high school play during his senior year. I think the drama class did something with Shakespeare."

"It wouldn't have been *The Tempest*, would it?"

"My memory isn't that good, Lou, but that certainly does have a familiar ring to it. How did you know?"

"Lucky guess, Brad."

"He was a good kid, Lou. Everyone thought he should have gone on to technical school, but there was no money for that. Selma was in no position to help. She couldn't even help Millie, which made her sick at heart. The boy's own family certainly wasn't going to help. They could have cared less about him. They never were there when he needed them, anyway.

"Selma treated the boy as if he was her son, and the boy loved his foster mother more than anyone in the world. Guess seeing what happened to her, what with all the medical bills and other problems she had, must have sent him over the edge. Way over!"

"My gut tells me he's on his way home, Brad. I think he did what he came East to do, and now, he's done. He's killed the three people who, in his mind, caused Selma the most pain.

"NYPD just put out an APB on him. But even knowing his name and having a photograph of him, a description of his car, and a license plate number, there's no assurance he'll get picked up between here and Iowa. Hell, he may have changed license plates or even cars by now. But again, I think he's heading home."

"I understand. So, what do you want to do at this point, Lou?"

"I'd like to make plans to take the first flight I can get out of New York or New Jersey early in the morning *the day after tomorrow* and fly into Des Moines. I want to see if he is picked up first. And I want to give you time to snoop around back there tomorrow, on the possibility he makes it back without being grabbed.

"If you can confirm, at the least, that he's back in your area, I'll fly out, grab a car at the airport, and drive to your office at Guthrie Center. We may have to bring the constable from Audubon County in on this, as well, depending on where the suspect is at the time. I'll leave that to you. Once we're together, you or the constable from Audubon County can attempt to take him into custody if you haven't already done so. I just want to be there. I want to look into his eyes. I have *never* met a killer who did the things this man did. I want to be there when he is taken down."

"I understand, Lou."

"Let me snoop around and determine whether or not he's returned to Audubon County, and if he has, whether he's returned to where he's been living or to where his car is registered. They could be different, you know. I'll also check around and see if I can find out where he works. Maybe a co-worker has seen him."

"See what you can learn, Brad. Meanwhile, I'll ask our assistant district attorney to talk to the people in Des Moines regarding extradition to New York. What do you think?"

"That should work. Let's hope he won't fight it. It'll make everything easier."

"You bet. Okay, look, I'll be in my office until 7 PM tonight. Remember, we're on Eastern Standard Time, but you always can call me on my cellphone after that. I'm going to go ahead and make plans to fly out the day after tomorrow on the assumption that our man will have returned to your area by then. Call me as soon as you can confirm that, even if it's in the middle of the night. For now, as far as I'm concerned, it's 'all systems go'. I always can reschedule my flight and rental car to accommodate whatever changes must be made."

"Will do, Lou. I'll call you as soon as I have something."

"By the way, Brad, how's Mrs. Holtzmann?"

"Not good. Doc Ewing gives her two days, three at the most. She's been on a morphine drip for the last several days. I think this is the end of her journey."

"I'm sorry, Brad."

"We're all sorry, Lou.

"I'll be talking to you."

Lou hung up the phone, shook his head, and then, dialed the NYPD Travel Office. It took only ten minutes for them to make his reservations out of New York's La Guardia Airport on Delta Air Lines, leaving at 6:10 AM, Eastern Standard Time the day after next. The flight, which had one stop, was scheduled to arrive at 9:32 AM Central Standard Time. Given the time needed to rent a car, Lou figured that he would be on his way by 10:15 AM, at the latest. He also asked his travel representative to make all the arrangements necessary with Delta and the Federal Air Marshall Service to expedite his boarding and obtain permission from the pilot so that he could carry his firearm onboard the aircraft.

With that accomplished, Lou spent the remainder of the day briefing his boss and several members of the City's Office of the District Attorney on his investigation. The attorneys stated that they would begin preparing immediately to take the case to the Grand Jury. It was their opinion that they would have no problem getting the nod to proceed with extradition of the suspect, once he was in the custody of either the Guthrie or Audubon County Constable. The possibility that the City of Washington, DC also would seek extradition of the suspect was discussed, so Lou, together with one of his City's attorneys, briefed DCPD Detective Jamar Jackson and several DC assistant district attorneys on NYPD's case and the identity of the suspect.

The representative from DC's Office of the District Attorney said they also would seek to extradite the suspect, once they were able to bring the matter before their Grand Jury. However, she said that her office probably would defer initially to New York City's Office of the District Attorney on the matter of extradition, given not only that the first homicide occurred there, but also, that two of the three murders were committed in New York City.

Twenty-six

'*L*ou, it's Brad!" The time was 1:27 AM. Stephanie rolled over, looked at the time displayed on her clock-radio, and went back to sleep. Lou got up, grabbed a pen and a notebook from his bedstand, hopped into the bathroom, shut the door, and turned on the light.

"Yeah, Brad. What's up?"

"He's back in the area, Lou. I just got a call from Bob Trimball, the constable in Audubon County. One of his patrolmen was called to a disturbance in a roadhouse on County Trunk Highway N14 a little before midnight tonight. He started talking to the bartender after things calmed down. She mentioned serving several beers around 11:30 PM to a guy who seemed pretty upset. According to the bartender, the man said he was going to kill anyone who hurt someone by the name of 'Selma'. The officer showed her our man's DMV photo, and she positively identified him. The Audubon County Police are looking for him now.

"If you still want to do it, Lou, I'd recommend you go ahead with your plans to fly out here later this morning. We'll work with Trimball to run our man to ground when you get here, assuming he and his people haven't arrested him up by the time you arrive."

"I'm coming out there, Brad. Nothing could hold me back. I'm packed. My airline ticket and rental car reservation are in my coat pocket.

"Man, I don't think I'll be able to sleep much more tonight, knowing what you just told me. You've done a terrific job. And please thank Constable Trimball and his people, if you would. That was real good police work."

"I'll do that, Lou.

"Now, let's both get some sleep. We have a busy day ahead of us."

"You bet! See you late in the morning, Brad."

Twenty-seven

*D*etective Lou Martelli's plane from New York's La Guardia Airport arrived in Des Moines, Iowa, on schedule. He deplaned quickly, and 30 minutes later, sat in his rental car, using his cellphone to let Stephanie know that he had arrived safely. By 10:30 AM, he had reached I-35N via Highway 5, where he turned north towards Grimes. There, he turned west on State Highway 44 for the trip to Guthrie Center.

Martelli was barely aware of what was playing on KJJY-FM, 92.5 MHz, a country-western station playing music that reminded him of his old friend, William "Bat" Masterson from Memphis and the great music Bill used to play at Camp Udairi in Kuwait before the invasion of Iraq . . . music by such artists as Alan Jackson, Lee Ann Womack and Willie Nelson, Faith Hill, Dolly Parton, and others. He and Bat used to sit and listen to Bat's CDs for hours at a time after a full day of flying Black Hawks on practice missions over the desert.

Bat always was the first one in line for mail call, but the men never knew whether it was because of the perfumed love letters he got from his wife or the country-western CDs she included with every letter.

Lou bit his lower lip thinking about those times. *Bill never made it back from Iraq,* he remembered. *I wonder whatever happened to his wife and their two boys.* He brushed a tear from his eye.

The ground still was covered with snow, but the highway was clear and the trip uneventful.

In town, Highway 44 became State Street. As was the case with almost every other town across America, this one, too, had succumbed to the 'homogenization' wrought by nationwide chains and franchises. Still, there was much to remind him of the country's history . . . of towns like this one that had spread across the prairie as its pioneer founders pushed west, by wagon train or railroad, to seek their fortunes. He slowed to a crawl, a pace better suited to enjoying the quietude that was missing from almost everything associated with his day-to-day life in Manhattan.

Coming to the center of town, he turned north on North 5th street, traveled a little over a block to 200 North 5th, and pulled into the parking lot across the street from the Municipal Building, a large, two-story red brick building with a decorative white-concrete facade. Pulling his overcoat around him, he walked to the building's front door and into the constable's office.

He was greeted by Officer Lake, who immediately sprang to his feet. The officer was a tall, self-assured man about 25 years old dressed in a starched, pressed uniform. He impressed Martelli as someone who could handle himself well in *any* situation. "You must be Detective Martelli. Constable Hutchinson said you'd be arriving about now. Talk about timing!"

"What do you mean, Officer?"

"There's shooting out at the Holtzmann farm. The constable's there now . . . pinned down, in fact, behind his patrol car. Two more patrol cars are there as well, but they're staying back . . . at the road. The constable told the other officers to hold their fire."

The Holtzmann farm! This can't be good, thought Lou. "Do you know what happened, Officer?"

"Yes, sir. The constable got a call from Terrell Holtzmann about twenty minutes ago. Doc Ewing had just pronounced Mrs. Holtzmann dead when this guy, Edward Cunningham—he was one of the foster kids that Selma and Karl took into their home—grabbed one of Terrell's hunting rifles and started talking crazy. Said he was going to kill everyone who had tried to stop the development of the drug Selma had been taking.

"Terrell and Doc Ewing beat it down the back stairs and out of the house . . . fast! They used Doc's cellphone to call the constable. That's when Constable Hutchinson strapped on his holster, put on his coat and hat, and told me to dispatch two patrol cars to meet him out there immediately. He said to send you to the farm as soon as you got here."

"What happened when he arrived?"

"Well, sir, Constable Hutchinson no sooner drove up to the front of the farmhouse when Cunningham opened fire. Damned if he didn't shoot out some of the roof-mounted strobe lamps on the constable's car just as he drove up. The guy must be a pretty good shot, that's for sure!

"Anyway, the constable dove over the car's console to the passenger side, opened the door, and managed to crawl to the ground. It took him several tries to release his rifle from its mount and grab some ammunition from inside the vehicle because Cunningham kept shooting at the car. But Constable Hutchinson finally managed to get his rifle and load it."

"Has he returned fire?"

"No. He just radioed that he wants to try talking Cunningham down from the bedroom on the second floor where he's barricaded himself. . .to take him into custody without harming him, if that's possible. The constable isn't one for shooting people if there's even the smallest chance that something can be resolved peaceful like."

"Okay, Officer. So, how do I get out there?"

"I made a map for you. It should be easy to follow. Go back to State Street and turn right, head out of town until you reach County Road N70, and then, head north. You can't miss the farm. You'll see Constable Hutchinson's white patrol car when you near the place, that's for sure."

"Thanks, Lake."

Martelli turned, awkwardly ran from the building as fast as he could, crossed the street, and hopped into his car. Backing out of his parking place, he slammed the car into 'D', gunned the engine, and sped out of the municipal parking lot towards State Street. There, he turned right, sped past Dowd Drug—'Established 1906'—and headed out of town on Highway 44.

Alternating between looking at the map and watching for the little white road signs that marked the county roads, he soon found the one marked 'N70'. Martelli 'stood' on the car's brakes, almost throwing the rear end of the car to the left, but giving him the ability to make the sharp right turn onto N70. *What the hell is going on up there now?* Lou could envision any number of scenarios.

He continued to push the speed limit, suddenly aware that patches of black ice covered the road's surface. The occasional

202

loss of traction and flashing electronic stability control indicator on his dashboard, showing that the car was transferring traction from one wheel to another, were a constant reminder that he could find himself in the ditch at any moment if he did not pay careful attention to the road. Still, with little time to spare, he pushed the car as fast as he dared.

It took ten minutes to reach the farm. As expected, the first thing he saw was the constable's patrol car. The red and blue roof-mounted strobe lights—or rather, what remained of them—were flashing. The right, front passenger door of the constable's car was open. He could see Brad Hutchinson crouched behind the engine compartment, bullhorn in hand. What appeared to be a high-powered rifle with scope was leaning against the right front fender.

Lou pulled behind two Guthrie County patrol cars that were parked with their engines running where the driveway leading to the Holtzmann farm met the county road. Lou identified himself to the two officers who were standing beside one of the vehicles. "Can I use your radio to talk to the constable?"

"Sure, Detective, use mine. One of the officers opened the driver's door on his patrol car, reached in, and withdrew his radio's microphone, which he handed to Lou. "Use this. We're all netted to the same frequency."

"Brad, this is Lou. Can you hear me?"

Lou saw the constable reach into his patrol car. A second later, the radio receiver's squelch broke, and he heard the constable's voice. "Welcome to Guthrie Center, Lou. Wish things had gone differently. We have a bad situation here."

"I can see that, Brad. Are you making progress?"

"No, can't say that I am. I can't even get him to talk to me. I've yelled through my bullhorn . . . even tried calling the house on the phone and letting it ring until *I* couldn't stand listening to it anymore. I simply can't get him to respond.

"And I don't want to shoot him. Truth be told, I could have dropped him several times in the last 10 minutes."

"What do you mean?"

"Well, the kid doesn't realize how vulnerable he is. Even if he stands to one side of the window, I still could put a bullet into him through the wood sash using my high-powered rifle. But I never killed anyone in my life, Lou, and don't aim to start now. I always prided myself on being able to resolve these situations in a more civilized manner."

"Brad, I want to come out there. I'm sure we can put our heads together and come up with something. Can you cover me?"

"Sure. Best if you use your rental. And no, I'm not trying to save the county money by preventing a second patrol car from falling victim to Cunningham's rifle. The guy's a good shot, I'll give him that. But I don't want him getting any more agitated than he already is by seeing another patrol car pulling into the front yard."

"Okay, when I begin edging into his field of fire, squeeze off a few rounds so that I can pull along side your car, behind where you're crouching."

"You got it. Be careful!"

Lou pulled his service revolver from the holster under his left shoulder, checked and reloaded the clip, set the safety, and put the weapon back in the holster. Then he got into his car, made a sharp right turn onto the pebble driveway leading to the house and barn, bumped his way across the stainless-steel cattle grid that was intended to prevent livestock from leaving the yard, and drove to the house. The white clapboard farmhouse with the large front porch and swing stood 300 feet back from the road. Behind it stood the red barn and concrete silo, both in need of paint. Lou could see a large pen filled with Guernsey cows off to one side. It was the quintessential country scene, unchanged from 60 or 70 years ago, and not unlike that found across the Great Heartland of America.

As he drove towards the constable's patrol car, he spotted it...a beat-up Chevy, brown, something from the late 1980s, with license plates issued for Audubon County. The first two numbers on the rear plate were '2' and '7'. *There it is...Cunningham's car,* he thought. *It's the car we saw in the videos.*

A shot rang out! Lou heard the bullet sear the roof of his rental car. *S#$%! Enterprise is going to be pissed. Where the hell is Brad? Why isn't he providing cover?*

Hearing Cunningham's shot, the constable opened fire, sending several rounds into the top of the window frame in the bedroom where Edward Cunningham had barricaded himself. *Better late than never,* Lou thought, skidding to a stop behind Brad, who by now had again crouched down behind the engine compartment of his patrol car.

Lou barely had time to open his door when another shot rang out, shattering his car's windshield and the right windshield post.

Lou threw open the door of his car, lay on his back, lifted his left leg out of the car, worked his right leg to the ground, and wiggled forward onto the gravel driveway.

"Damn, Brad, this isn't quite the way I figured this would end."

"Nor I. I never figured Cunningham for a killer. I did a little snooping around yesterday. Best I was able to determine, when his plans to attend technical school didn't pan out, he just drifted from one low-level job to another. He's currently working at the meat packing plant in Audubon as a Master Butcher. His co-workers told me he's one of the best they've ever seen."

Another shot rang out, this one destroying what remained of the strobe flashers mounted on the constable's patrol car.

"That's one angry young man, Brad. And knowing what I learned from my investigation, I think I can understand what he must be feeling. Do you mind if I try talking to him?"

The constable handed Martelli the bullhorn. "Couldn't hurt. I'm certainly not getting anywhere with him."

Lou took the bullhorn, slowly poked his head above the engine compartment, and was just about to speak when yet another shot rang out. He heard the bullet whistle overhead. *Is this guy intentionally aiming high, or am I just lucky?* Lou thought.

Lou looked at the damaged roof-mounted strobe flashers on the constable's patrol car.

"This isn't going to work, Brad." Before the constable knew what was happening, Lou took off his shoulder holster, dropped it to the ground, threw his hands into the air—one of which held his badge—and limped out from behind the patrol car.

"Edward Cunningham, I'm Detective Louis Martelli, New York Police Department."

The countryside echoed with the sound of yet another rifle shot from Cunningham's rifle. Like the previous round, Lou heard the bullet whistle over his head. He didn't flinch.

Lou stood his ground. "Don't shoot, Edward!" *If he was going to kill me,* Lou thought, *he would have done it by now. No, he's not going to kill me, but when Stephanie finds out about this, SHE will!*

Lou stood perfectly still, his hands still high in the air. "Edward, I'm unarmed." Lou lowered his arms slowly and opened his overcoat and suit jacket to show Cunningham that he had no shoulder or belt holsters. He lifted his pants cuffs to show that he was not wearing an ankle holster. "See! I have no weapons. I just want to talk with you."

"What happened to your leg?" The question came from the upstairs window of the farmhouse.

"Oh, that! It was just a little accident, Edward."

"Looks like it was more than 'just a little accident', Detective."

"Well, I was a passenger in a vehicle that was involved in an accident. I'm afraid my leg was among the 'casualties'."

"Does it hurt?"

"Not anymore. But I'll tell you something odd. I get these phantom sensations from time to time. Occasionally, it feels like my toes are tingling. But of course, they can't be. They're gone. But it's not a problem."

"Weird, man."

"I'll say! By the way, mind if I put my hands down and come just a little closer? My arms are getting tired, and I can't keep shouting in this cold weather. I'm getting hoarse."

There was no answer. Lou put his arms down and limped five steps closer to the front porch. He could hear his father's silver dollars jingling in his pocket.

"Edward, I know why you killed those people in New York City and Washington. I know what you were thinking."

207

Still no answer. And then, though Lou could not see anyone in the window, he saw the lower sash of the upstairs bedroom window open wider. "What do you mean 'You know why I did what I did'? How does anyone know what I was thinking?"

Lou took a few more steps towards the farmhouse. "I know because I have been looking into the backgrounds of the people you murdered, both in New York and Washington. What I found made me sick! I couldn't believe how Wall Street not only was manipulating the price of Berranger's stock, but also, working to undermine the approval of the drug that Selma was taking. And to make matters worse, neither the SEC nor the FDA seemed to care . . . even when people called their attention to what was happening! Even Congress wouldn't do anything."

"All Wall Street cares about is the money, Detective, I understand that. But what about the doctors? Whatever happened to 'First, do no harm'? How can doctors, who should be trying to *save* lives, work to defeat the approval of a drug that appears to do just that? It makes no sense."

"Actually, it does, Edward. My father, God rest his soul, taught me that when something doesn't make sense, follow the money. Once you do that, he used to say, it shouldn't take long before everything becomes abundantly clear."

"I guess so. After reading Millie's articles in the Des Moines newspapers, there was no question in my mind who was behind Berranger's problems. When no one did anything about them, I decided I had to act."

"I know, Edward. My people saw what was going on within the FDA and how the SEC was asleep at the switch when it came to looking into what the brokerage houses and others were doing.

We've gathered an extensive amount of material that New York City's Office of the District Attorney will turn over to the New York Attorney General. From there, the material probably will be turned over to the US Department of Justice."

"But will they do anything? Does anybody in Washington care that Wall Street is killing people? I mean, this has been going on for years. No one cares. People write letters to the SEC. . . to Congress. Nothing happens. When is all this going to stop? *Who's going to make it stop?*"

"I don't know the answer to that question, Edward. But killing more people isn't going to help the situation. Look, let's say you killed me. You'd never get out of here alive. In the end, the press only would focus on you as a murderer. They wouldn't pay much attention at all to what happened to Selma or Berranger. And what would that accomplish?"

"So, what's the alternative?"

"The alternative is to come down here and let Constable Hutchinson take you back to Guthrie Center. Eventually, you're going to have to return to New York City and face trial for the murders of John Williamson and Dr. Demetri Mihailov. And at some time in the future, you'll also have to stand trial in Washington, DC, for the murder of Dr. Paul Broussard.

"Meanwhile, Millie Fergesen will tell your story. I can promise you that she will. And when she's finished, every adult in the United States will understand Wall Street's manipulative practices and how the US financial markets and the pharmaceutical industry have 'captured' their regulators."

There was no response.

Lou looked back at Brad, who was drawing a bead on the upstairs bedroom window. Brad shrugged. "Don't look at me, Lou. I don't know what the boy has up his sleeve."

Lou limped forward and was about to put his right foot on the first step of the stairs when he heard the hinges on the farmhouse door squeak.

Lou froze.

Hutchinson took aim with his rifle at the door and ever so gently tightened his finger around the trigger.

"Don't shoot! Don't shoot!" Cunningham yelled, as he opened the door just enough to throw the rifle he had been using onto the porch. Then, very slowly, he emerged from the farmhouse with both hands in the air.

Lou looked at the man he had been chasing. At the top of the stairs he saw a husky, six-foot-tall country boy with sandy, tousled hair, wearing glasses, torn jeans, and a red flannel shirt missing several buttons. His cowboy boots were shoddy and scuffed, and he looked exhausted, as if he had not slept in days. But he seemed at peace, as if a terrible burden had just been lifted from his shoulders.

The constable brushed by Lou, ran up the stairs, and cuffed Cunningham's hands behind his back. Then, using his right hand, the constable gripped the young man's left arm tightly and walked him down the stairs to where Lou was standing.

They stopped at the bottom. Cunningham looked at Lou with mournful eyes. "I'm terribly sorry for all the trouble I've caused you, Detective."

Lou looked at him, nodded, but said nothing. Then, he turned around, and as he limped back to his rental car, dialed Millie Fergesen's office number on his cellphone.

Epilogue

*E*dward Cunningham waived extradition from Iowa and was returned to New York City. He currently is being held in Rikers Island, pending trial for the murders of John Williamson and Demetri Mihailov, MD. He still faces extradition to the District of Columbia to stand trial for the murder of Dr. Paul Broussard.

Despite a positive, late-summer advisory committee meeting at which panel members *recommended approval* of Berranger Biotechnology Systems' *HerDeciMax* for the treatment of HER2-positive breast cancer (the votes were 15-1 that the drug was safe, and 14-2 that it provided substantial evidence of efficacy), the FDA *refused* to approve the drug. Rumor had it that the Chemo Cartel's stranglehold on the FDA 'killed' any chance that such a revolutionary new treatment would be approved anytime in the near future. Berranger's stock price fell below $1 per share, and the company was delisted from the Over-The-Counter (OTC) Market. Dr. Smithson, Founder and President of Berranger, tendered his resignation from the corporation, which was accepted reluctantly by its board of directors. The board currently is in discussions to merge Berranger with another biotechnology corporation. Dr. Smithson, meanwhile,

211

has received backing from two venture capital firms. He is in the process of forming a new corporation to explore the development of small molecules for the treatment of various cancers, including ovarian cancer.

The Phase III trial of BCaPharmaceutical's new drug, *BCa-1407* for breast cancer, failed to achieve its primary endpoint, as stipulated in the company's agreement with the FDA. The drug was shown to be safe and well tolerated, but the data remained insufficient to prove its efficacy. According to the company, the trial will continue for another year so that additional data can be collected for analysis. The shares of BCaPharmaceutical dropped by more than 50% on the news. The company now is the target of a hostile takeover by two European pharmaceutical giants looking to augment their product lines with BCaPharmaceutical's products.

The Enforcement Division of the Securities and Exchange Commission, despite being provided with the data acquired by the New York Police Department via the City's Office of the District Attorney and the New York Attorney General, never opened an investigation into the activities of the research arm of Bartlett, Cline, and Stephenson. Nor has the agency taken any meaningful steps to rein in naked short selling and other market abuses by hedge funds and 'dark pools' of liquidity. Lending credence to this observation and to the almost total incompetence and impotence of the agency was its inability to control, much less explain, the stock market's plunge on May 6, 2010, when the Dow Jones Industrial Average dropped almost 1,000 points.[37]

---

37 http://www.theepochtimes.com/n2/content/view/34886/ About $700 billion of U.S. stock market value was erased in less than 10 minutes.

The Food and Drug Administration, while it has tightened requirements pertaining to waivers in cases where conflicts of interest exist, still has not taken the steps necessary to resolve the full range of issues that must be addressed in his area.

Detective Louis Martelli was awarded the NYPD's highest Commendation for Excellence by the mayor of New York in a ceremony attended by his family and co-workers. He was promoted to Detective-Investigator at the same ceremony.

Missy Dugan was promoted to Supervisor, Information Technology Laboratory, NYPD, and given a significant bonus for the part she played in helping Detective Louis Martelli solve the Williamson and Mihailov murders.

Tricia Fournier is institutionalized in New York City at Bellevue Hospital Center. There is little hope she ever will regain her sanity.

Millie Fergesen was promoted to Managing Editor, the *Plains Courier,* Des Moines, Iowa, in September, 2010. She was the first woman to hold this post. The promotion was in recognition of her nationally syndicated series of stories on the murders of John Williamson, Dr. Paul Broussard, and Demetri Mihailov, MD. The nation was horrified to learn that the killings and subsequent dismemberment of the bodies were most likely acts of revenge for actions taken by the murder victims to stop the approval by the FDA of Berranger's *HerDeciMax* treatment for HER2-positive breast cancer.

Constable Hutchinson was unopposed for re-election. His role in the capture of Edward Cunningham was featured in newspapers throughout the State, and the governor of Iowa presented him with a plaque, honoring him for meritorious service to the community.

Former US Army Sergeant Luke Sanders, who served during the Viet Nam War with Charlie Company of 1st Battalion, 20th Infantry Regiment, 11th Brigade, 23rd Infantry Division, is receiving assistance from the US Department of Veterans Affairs. He is making progress towards a full recovery.

Terrell Holtzmann married his high school sweetheart, Amy Nelson, in May, 2010. They continue to work the Holtzmann family farm north of Guthrie Center, Iowa.

Theodore J. Cohen, PhD, holds three degrees in the physical sciences from the University of Wisconsin–Madison and has been an engineer and scientist for more than 40 years. He has been an investor since 1960, focusing almost entirely since 1980 on the world of biotechnology. His experience spans the dawn of the Age of Biotechnology in the late 1970's to today's era of ever more impactful successes in the field. *Death by Wall Street: Rampage of the Bulls,* is his first novel pertaining to the fields of investing and biotechnology. Dr. Cohen also has published more than 350 papers, articles, columns, essays, and interviews in the fields of communications and electronics, and is a co-author of *The NEW Shortwave Propagation Handbook* from CQ Communications. His first novel, *Full Circle: A Dream Denied, A Vision Fulfilled,* which is based on life as a violinist— Dr. Cohen plays with the Bryn Athyn (PA) Orchestra—was published by AuthorHouse in 2009. He also has written three novels that comprise his Antarctic Murders Trilogy: *Frozen in Time: Murder at the Bottom of the World* (Book I); *Unfinished Business: Pursuit of an Antarctic Killer* (Book II); and *End Game: Irrational Acts, Tragic Consequences* (Book III; to be published in fall, 2010). The Trilogy is available from AuthorHouse, as well. From December 1961 through early March 1962, Dr. Cohen participated in the 16th Chilean Expedition to the Antarctic. The US Board of Geographic Names in October, 1964, named the geographical feature Cohen Islands, located at 63° 18' S. latitude, 57° 53' W. longitude in the Cape Legoupil area, Antarctica, in his honor. Dr. Cohen served in the US Army Corps of Engineers from March 1966 through March 1968, leaving the service with the rank of Captain.

Breinigsville, PA USA
30 November 2010
250310BV00001B/17/P